M000029426

LAW AND DISORDER

LAW AND DISORDER

MAGIC CITY CHRONICLES™ BOOK SIX

TR CAMERON   MICHAEL ANDERLE   MARTHA CARR

DISRUPTIVE IMAGINATION

This book is a work of fiction. All of the characters, organizations, and events portrayed in this novel are either products of the author's imagination or are used fictitiously. Sometimes both.

Copyright © 2021 LMBPN Publishing
Cover by Fantasy Book Design
Cover copyright © LMBPN Publishing
A Michael Anderle Production

LMBPN Publishing supports the right to free expression and the value of copyright. The purpose of copyright is to encourage writers and artists to produce the creative works that enrich our culture.

The distribution of this book without permission is a theft of the author's intellectual property. If you would like permission to use material from the book (other than for review purposes), please contact support@lmbpn.com. Thank you for your support of the author's rights.

LMBPN Publishing
PMB 196, 2540 South Maryland Pkwy
Las Vegas, NV 89109

Version 1.00 June, 2021
ebook ISBN: 978-1-64971-825-9
Print ISBN: 978-1-64971-826-6

The Oriceran Universe (and what happens within / characters / situations / worlds) are Copyright (c) 2017-21 by Martha Carr and LMBPN Publishing.

THE LAW AND DISORDER TEAM

Thanks to the JIT Readers

Wendy L Bonell
Dorothy Lloyd
John Ashmore
Larry Omans
Dave Hicks
Diane L. Smith
Paul Westman

If I've missed anyone, please let me know!

Editor
Skyhunter Editing Team

DEDICATION

For those who seek wonder around every corner and in each turning page. Thank you choosing to share the adventure with me. And, as always, for Dylan and Laurel.

— *TR Cameron*

CHAPTER ONE

The comm in her ear came jarringly to life in the quiet of the night. Kayleigh, the tech with the callsign "Glam," announced, "Drones show no activity." *That's not useful,* Ruby thought snarkily. After several training sessions to better integrate with Diana Sheen's agents, she, Idryll, and Morrigan were in the field for their first real operation alongside them. Ruby and Idryll were teamed up with Cara Binot and Anik Khan, "Croft" and "Khan," respectively. Diana, Rath, Morrigan, and Tony Ryan were functioning as a separate unit and currently holding a position across the target compound from them.

The place was allegedly a religious commune, and Demetrius's research showed it to be a legitimate nonprofit with sites in several states. This one was also a front for the black-market-magic-item-trade, including the Rhazdon artifacts Diana's team was interested in. Ruby absently rubbed her arm through her costume, directly over the spot where the artifact that had embedded itself into her body rested. She was doing a better job of keeping its voice at bay, thanks to training from Diana's Drow mentor Nylotte, but she still worried about it frequently. *At least it's not a constant worry anymore. Baby steps.*

Diana said, "Thermal scans?"

Glam replied, "Same as the last time you asked, Boss. A couple in each building, far fewer than our surveillance spotted entering during the day."

Morrigan observed, "So, this is a front and they portaled to a different location?"

Ruby shrugged. "Maybe. Or could be it's something simpler." She reached behind her to the compartment on her belt that held the tiny drone, retrieved it, and set the vehicle on the ground. Margrave had upgraded the control system, which was now a cuff she wore as part of her costume. Only the thin silver ring encircling the tip of her right index finger could activate its touchscreen display. She launched the craft and switched it into rotating detection modes. It would look for sound, thermal, electricity, and even sense the presence of magic, although that last one was still a work in progress since its range was dismal. "Glam, my drone is out."

The tech replied, "On it." A moment later, her local view of the drone's camera in her mask's eyepiece converted to a feed from the agents' headquarters showing the same thing but shared among the entire team. She piloted it close to the nearest Quonset hut, one of four curved buildings arrayed without apparent logic on the property. As it *swished* along the side, the rotors chopping mostly ineffectively at the tall grass, the thermal image displayed a smear of color. She tapped the command to lock onto that detection mode and put the drone into a hover. The display showed blobs moving where there were none to be seen.

Diana said, "Underground. Makes sense. The Quonset huts are big enough to hide any evidence of their excavation, assuming there weren't tunnels there already. They probably have a defense inside to resist thermal sensing, but they couldn't spread it everywhere, so your drone was able to pick up something ours higher up couldn't."

Glam growled, "I've been telling you we need to upgrade the drones."

Diana snorted. "*I've* been telling *you* we need to put our time and energy into other things, not to mention our limited funds." Ruby didn't know much about the team that called themselves the Federal Agents of Magic but wasn't surprised to hear that the government didn't provide them with an overly abundant amount of operating capital.

In a tone that conveyed the continuation of a long-running conversation, the tech replied, "*That's* why we need to start liberating some valuable items from adventures like this and selling them off the books. Or turn them in for rewards. Either way."

Khan sighed loudly. "That would be highly unethical, and you know it."

Glam countered, "So says the guy who makes his living inflicting property damage in large amounts. When I picture you during operations, you're always carrying one of those cartoonish black sphere bombs with a lit fuse sticking out of the top. You're doing it right now, aren't you? Admit it."

Diana cut the chatter short. "Don't insult Khan. You

know how he gets hurt when you make fun of his toys. My team will enter the Quonset hut nearest us. Croft, take yours into the one closest to you. We go in one minute from mark." A countdown appeared in Ruby's display. At first, it had been difficult getting used to having data from the tech appear unexpectedly on a lens of her mask, but now it seemed completely normal.

She patted her equipment for at least the tenth time since they'd crawled into position a half-hour before. Bulletproof vest, pistol, extra magazines, dart gun around her forearm, daggers at her hips, and her sword across her back. The throwing knives never left her boots except when targeted at an enemy, so there was no need to check them. She touched the flasks on her chest and thigh pouch containing healing and energy potions. From beside her, Idryll asked, "Did you lose anything since you last checked five minutes ago?"

Ruby scowled at her companion. The shapeshifter seemed to relish making fun of her when Diana's people were on comms. "Shut it, you, or I'll drop your disguise so everyone targets you first." Ruby maintained an illusion that made her and the tiger-woman look like the agents, who wore masks in addition to their standard gear. Morrigan would be doing the same. *No reason to let our enemies know that the protectors of Magic City are part of tonight's adventure.*

Although technically the compound was a little out of their jurisdiction, an hour's drive away from Ely, Ruby wouldn't miss a chance to be involved in anything artifact-related until she figured out a way to master the thing in her arm or remove it. *Unfortunately, since the only proven method of separating oneself from a Rhazdon artifact is dying, my options for the latter aren't looking all that good.* Idryll had suggested they could cut off the limb and see if that did the trick and offered to wield the sword to do it, but Ruby wasn't quite ready to give that a try, either.

Croft ordered, "I'm first, then Jewel, then Cat, then Khan." Glam was responsible for their new codenames, and they fit well. Morrigan's was Barb, a reference to the wicked hooks on some of the arrows she carried. Deacon's voice popped up now and again in service of his role handling the technical aspects of the run, other than surveillance, which was Glam's purview.

When the clock ran out, they dashed forward to the Quonset hut and put their backs against the wall next to the door. Croft nodded, and Khan moved to the doors and yanked on a handle. "Locked, but not for long." He pushed a small rectangle onto the seam above the handles and took a step away. It detonated with a soft *pop*, and the doors swung freely. He grabbed one and pulled it open, and Ruby followed Croft into the dimly lit space.

As the heat signatures from Glam's drone had indicated, a pair of occupants were inside. Both were in motion, rising from chairs set at a round table that held a deck of cards and two bottles of Coke. Individual cards drifted toward the ground as the two men snatched guns holstered at their waists. As they'd arranged in advance, Croft darted forward to the one on the left and used her left hand to prevent him from bringing the gun to bear and delivered a right cross to his temple. A loud *snap* sounded as the agent's stun glove discharged, and her opponent dropped.

Ruby wasn't wearing gloves, but she did have low-profile metal knuckles over her right hand, which she'd charged to full before heading out for the operation. Margrave had designed them to deliver just enough power to take out a human, so when she drove her punch into the man's nose, it smashed the cartilage and knocked him unconscious. Idryll complained, "You could've left one of them for me."

Croft ordered, "Find the way down." The others moved to examine the floor of the building, which seemed to be irregular layers of cheap plywood stacked a few deep. Ruby piloted her drone inside and ran it around the space, seeking telltales. It was Khan who found it, noting that a piece of the floor creaked a little more than the rest as he walked over it. A quick search revealed an exceedingly thin gap in the wood, covered by a clever disguise. They pried it up and discovered a ladder descending a hewn rock chimney. Croft snapped a glow stick and threw it into the opening, revealing the end of the vertical shaft twenty feet below. "Let's do it." She jumped, doubtless planning to use magic to break her fall.

Idryll sighed. "You have an incredibly agile and profoundly bored member of your team who could do that jump without magic, but do you send her first? No, of course not."

Ruby clapped her on the back. "I'm sure there will be plenty of fun for everyone."

Diana's voice came over the comm. "We're underground. Be wary. The approaches are trapped."

There was a *sizzle* and a *snap* from below, but no other response. Ruby asked, "Croft?"

The absence of a reply shot anxiety through her. Khan said, "Go to it, Cat. Be careful. Maybe use the ladder." Before he'd finished the sentence, Idryll had leapt down after their team leader.

CHAPTER TWO

Ruby followed Idryll down and found Croft waiting for them at the bottom. The agent said, "There was a stun trap down here. My magic set it off, so it didn't get me, but it fried my comm." Ruby reported that information to Khan, who was still on his way down and heard him share it with Diana. The agents' leader said, "Okay, Khan, you're in charge. Tell Croft she's paying for the replacement comm. Let me guess. She jumped instead of climbing down the ladder."

Khan laughed. "Got it in one."

Diana's response was amused. "True to form. I love that about her. Okay, the sensors in my suit aren't giving me much, but it looks like there's a tunnel in front of me."

He hopped down the last couple rungs and replied, "Same here." The data filled in as a wireframe map on Ruby's eyepiece. "Not getting anything from very far away either, though."

"Assume there will be traps. Move quickly, but safely. What direction is yours in?"

"North-northwest."

After a second's pause, Glam said, "If the tunnels are reasonably straight, that should bring you both toward the same location."

Diana replied, "Makes sense. Okay, let's get moving."

Diana connected her comm exclusively to Morrigan. "Barb, you all good?"

"One hundred percent."

"Excellent." She switched to the party channel. "Rambo, you have the best senses here. Go scout."

The troll, wearing his custom version of their battle armor with the rectangular case holding his mechanical wings strapped on his back, chirped, "Right on, Boss," and advanced warily. "Traps. Why did there have to be traps?"

Diana sighed. "You've been using that *Raiders of the Lost Ark* quote way too often lately. I think you need to watch more movies."

"The classics always work." They moved forward through the dimly lit passage, the illumination coming from LED lanterns hanging from above. The roof of the corridor was only a couple of inches above her head, so she had to swerve out of the way of the lighting instruments whenever they appeared. Rath, in his three-foot form, had no problems with them. She froze as he said, "Stop."

"Physical or magical?"

"Physical at least. The dust is disturbed, but I don't see anything."

Diana looked where he was pointing and waited while

her display cycled through detection modes, revealing nothing. She crouched and extended her magical senses, looking for a clue. "Okay, there's something arcane there. I'm guessing it's an illusion, but a pretty sophisticated one. I wouldn't want to set off the trap by dispelling it." She connected to the other team and warned them of what she'd found, then added, "Let's try that old Indiana Jones trick."

She scraped her glove along the ground, gathering up dust, then rose and threw it forward in a line that extended from the floor to the ceiling. At about shin level, the particles were disturbed by something. She reported over the comm, "Looks like a magical tripwire. We'll try going over it. Rath, you're the most agile. Have at it." In the past, she'd been a little overprotective of her troll life partner. After their headquarters in Pittsburgh blew up and they'd relocated to the vimana, he'd spent an impressive amount of time training with anyone who would teach him things and was now the equal of any of them.

To be honest, given his ability to grow into a seven-foot version with muscles that would put a bodybuilding champion to shame, probably better than most of us. She watched as he carefully examined the ground beyond the tripwire before flowing into a somersault leap with no apparent windup. He landed cleanly on the opposite side, and she held her breath, waiting. Nothing happened, and the rest of the team followed, though generally less acrobatically. "Going over it worked. I'll let you know if we find another one."

Khan replied, "Affirmative." They had found their tripwire, and he carefully led the way over it. After, he asked, "Jewel, have anything that will help here?"

Ruby answered, "Not really. I can create an illusory version of us, but it's not a physical thing. It would only set off traps that involve cameras or maybe sound if I made them noisy. Never actually tried that before."

He shook his head. "I haven't spotted any cameras, and no electrical lines run through here, so I presume the outer perimeter devices we defeated on our way in were the only electronic surveillance. Let's keep that option in reserve."

They continued forward, and Ruby sensed growing anxiety in her partner. She whispered, "Idryll, what's up?"

The shapeshifter frowned. "I sense danger, that's all. I don't know why, and I don't know from where."

They navigated two more of the invisible tripwires before the passage changed, widening out ten feet ahead. Khan stopped them and warned, "Moments of transition like this are always good spots for trouble. Especially right before the changeover." He spoke with the confidence of long experience rigging traps. As the agents' primary demolition man, such things were his specialty. He led them into the larger space cautiously, everyone scanning the walls, floors, and ceiling for dangers.

When they were all inside, an unexpected set of metal bars dropped into place in front of and behind them. They all crouched, seeking additional threats. The sound of hissing announced the dispersal of gas into their area. *Thank goodness our masks filter out hazardous chemicals.* Ruby felt good about that for almost an entire second before Khan observed, "That's gasoline vapor."

The tunnel widened ahead, and Diana took the lead position from Rath. She sent the other agent, Tony Ryan to the back. She gripped the rifle hanging from the strap at her chest and pointed it forward, then moved forward in a slow crouch, walking heel to toe and keeping her balance centered. The comms fell suddenly silent, the hiss of the open channel that was their constant companion absent. Ryan said, "Jamming. Working on it." He was responsible for local tech and operated effectively even without Glam and Deacon backing him up.

She replied, "We can't wait. Keep moving." She spotted the openings in the wall an instant before the bars tried to slam out and trap them. Dropping her rifle, she summoned force magic and pushed back, holding them immobile. "Go through quickly." The strain against her power wasn't an immediate problem, but she couldn't restrain the barriers forever, either. When the others were through, she released the rear one, moved out of the planned trap, and let the other go. As it locked into place, gas hissed from vents in the ceiling. She led her team farther down the tunnel, then turned thoughtfully. "Automatic trap, or did someone deploy it?"

Rath replied, "I didn't see a trigger."

Morrigan said, "Me neither, so maybe they turned on the jamming to hide the system of cameras or whatever they're using?"

She nodded. "Possible. Let's not disappoint them." She summoned an orb of fire in her hand and threw it at the bars. When it met the gas, it exploded in a fiery conflagration. "Hopefully, that'll confuse them. Time to move."

Ruby created a gust of wind and blew the gas through the metal fence and back along the tunnel. "Don't know if they were trying to suffocate us, incinerate us, or whatever, but let's not find out. Idryll, can you do something with those bars?"

The shapeshifter nodded. The rails were fairly far apart, and a few more inches on each side would give them room to squeeze through. She performed the partial transformation Ruby had watched her often practicing in the recent past, adding the musculature of her tiger form to parts of her body while holding onto the benefits of leverage and, well, *hands* her humanoid physique offered. She strained at the bars, and Ruby envisioned a horizontal line of force between them, calling the magic into being and attempting to widen it, adding more pressure to the vertical rails. They parted with a groan, and the team went through cautiously, one by one. Khan said, "The time for subtlety seems to be at an end. Let's do this."

They charged forward in a line, and when the tunnel ended in a door, Ruby used force magic to blast off its hinges and send it into the room without breaking stride. They entered a large space, roughly rectangular, that looked like it had been chopped out of the stone by physical labor. It was home to a half-dozen tables with surprised-looking beings around them, as well as a bunch of guards. She noted two other entrances to the chamber, a broad set of double doors to her left and one identical to their entry portal ahead of her. That one banged open an instant later to reveal the other team moving at speed into the area.

Ruby strengthened her shields, drew her pistol, and yelled, "Everyone down and no one gets hurt."

Predictably, not one of them dropped to the floor. Instead, half of the group started to grab things off the tables while the other half moved to attack the invaders, particularly the one who had shouted at them a moment before. *Why doesn't anyone ever listen to me?*

CHAPTER THREE

Diana noted the other team's presence across the room, but the scene inside caught her attention. A dozen magicals were on the move to repel their invasion, and about that number were grabbing stuff off the tables and shoving it into bags or bins. She snapped, "Barb, engage anyone at range. Stark, you stay back. Make sure they don't escape through these tunnels. Rambo, you have right. I'll take center." She had to shout the words because the jamming was still interfering with their comms.

Mental note, have Glam and Deacon figure out how they compromised our communication and ensure it never happens again. She lifted her rifle and squeezed off three bullets at the lead enemy. The elf summoned a magical shield, but the anti-magic rounds ignored it on their way to lodging in his chest and shoulder. His last-minute flinch saved him from her center mass aim, but he was out of the fight. *If he doesn't get quick medical attention, he'll soon be out of everything.* Diana recalled moments in her career where she'd felt concern and remorse about such events. Now, after her team gave a warning, she considered combat damage simply the result of a foe's poor choices and slept soundly afterward.

To her right, Rath hurled knives at high speed, depleting all six of his daggers in twice that many seconds. They flew true, and while they succeeded in impaling the first enemy he targeted, the second summoned a shield to block them. She traversed her aim to the next target, then had to dive aside as one of the tables hurtled forward directly in between her and her objective. *Dammit, they coped with the anti-magic bullets much faster than I would've liked.* She dropped the rifle to hang from its strap and drew her sword, Fury's battle cry echoing in her head. She charged at the one who threw the table at her, a dwarf with a nasty scar wearing an expression to match.

Morrigan had few targeting options, given the general melee that was developing. She let the first arrow fly in a shallow arc over the heads of the front ranks. It landed in the back of the chamber, smacking one of the people fleeing toward the room's rear exit. The impact only caused her target to stumble forward, but when the knockout gas spread, that person fell. Another was quick on the uptake, casting a spell to move the vapor away, smartly sending it back at the nearest attacker. *If we weren't wearing masks, that play might have been effective.*

Her fingers had already found the next arrow in her quiver, and she fitted it to the string and loosed it. It slammed into the rear wall, discharging vibrations that would mess with the inner ear of anyone in a six-foot semi-circle. She assumed the stone would stop it from penetrating beyond the room but had never tested to see. *Another item for the to-do list.* Its effects were immediate, and those nearest stumbled and fell to the floor as their sense of balance abandoned them. The power cell in the arrow was only good for about ten seconds, but it would be enough to keep a few people out of the fight during its active stage and for however long it took them to regain their equilibrium after.

Her fingers brushed against an explosive arrow, but she decided that would be literal overkill in such a small space. Instead, she chose one of the sharpened arrows that had inspired her call sign and searched the battlefield for the most powerful-looking enemy who wasn't currently paying attention to her. She found a hulking Kilomea that had been standing guard against the back wall and was now charging into the melee. An instant later, the missile was speeding toward him.

Idryll had charged forward as soon as the enemy had moved. She concentrated to maintain some extra strength in her arms and torso, not as much as she'd needed to bend the bars, but sufficient to give her an additional edge in the fight. *Not that I really need another edge.* She extended her claws, the sharp talons coming out of her fingertips, and leapt with a shout toward the closest elf. He summoned a fast shield that wasn't strong enough to stop her completely, and she scored a trio of bloody furrows along his cheek. Only his last-minute twist saved the eye she'd targeted. She stabbed the other hand in at his sternum, but he blocked down with a hard strike, numbing her fingers. It was only when the knee crashed into her stomach ahead of her instinctive block that she realized he had amplified his speed. She straightened from her reflexive protective curve and retreated into a fighting stance to await his next attack.

It didn't take long to arrive. His combat style was quick and short-range, intended to offer an opponent the smallest possible amount of time to react to his incredibly fast strikes. She let her thoughts go and trusted instinct, and her claws sliced along both of his arms as she deflected punches that were almost too swift to see. She caught a rising kick on her foot and spun as soon as she returned it to the ground, bringing a heel around toward his head. He dropped to avoid it and punched her knee.

Idryll twisted enough that the joint didn't break, but the leg collapsed underneath her. She rolled in that direction and came up quickly, jamming her leg backward in a back kick. It caught the incoming elf and knocked him back a step. She set that foot down and spun, feinting another kick and bringing her fist around at temple height. His effort to deflect it was too slow, and he flew sideways from the force of the amplified blow, no longer a threat.

She pointed across the chamber at one of the two Kilomea who had been flanking the rear doors when they'd entered. He nodded and beckoned her forward, drawing a long ax from a sheath on his back. *I do so love a good playmate.*

Ruby still hadn't developed the instinct of going for her gun first, and by the time her brain thought of it, furniture was already flying through the room as a physical barrier to defend against the anti-magic rounds. In the interim, she had whipped a line of force at the nearest enemy, wrapped it around his feet, and yanked it hard to drop him onto his back. A stream of flame followed immediately after, but the elf had the presence of mind to summon a shield to intercept it. She charged toward the center of the chamber, leaving him for someone else to finish.

The clatter of a grenade accompanied by billowing smoke signaled Khan's entry into the fight, and Croft was already halfway through the space, daggers in her hands as she raced at a pair of defenders who were falling back toward the rear doors. It had quickly become evident that members of the enemy group were heading through that exit, carrying items away that probably included the artifacts they sought. Ruby used a force blast to launch herself into the air, fully intending to sail over the fray using the two-story height of the chamber to her advantage. It was not to be, however. A gnome employed her tactics against her by wrapping a line of shadow around her ankles and jerking her toward the ground.

The touch of the dark power woke the artifact in her arm, and its chatter in her mind urged her to put it to use, offered help with no strings. *Right. As if.* She pushed the idea aside as she used force magic to cushion her impact on the stone floor. Ruby rolled and sent a stuttering blast of fire darts at the gnome, forcing him to summon a shield and abandon the shadow rope around her ankles. She drew her sword in one hand and her dagger in the other as she rose, and used the latter to call up a shield to intercept the shadow bolts he threw at her face.

For a moment, they remained motionless, regarding each other. He was of average height for his species and wore a vest full of bulging pockets. A screwdriver handle stuck out of one, and she wondered if he was a techno-mancer like her and Margrave. She decided it was some-thing to check out later because that might have implications for the bigger picture and charged him. By the time she crossed the distance, he had summoned a large staff made of force, with a wicked edge along the top and bottom portions. It was a magical weapon of the type she'd never seen before, most analogous to a double-ended spear. It gave him the reach his size took away, and he spun the object with more skill and strength than she would've expected.

Ruby deflected the first swing with a raised sword, but he quickly disengaged it and stabbed at her eyes, again much more skillfully than predicted. She took a step back-ward and yanked her head back to avoid it, then threw out a force blast intended to knock him off his feet. He let go of the spear with one hand and cast a spell to nullify hers without breaking the rotational pattern of his defense. *Damn, the little guy's good. Not good enough though, unless he has eyes in the back of his head.*

She reached out with her force magic, grabbed one of the tables already in midair, and pulled. The gnome—who was halfway between her and the object—lost his grip on the spear at its impact and stumbled forward in an uncontrolled rush. Her knee snapped to meet his head as he came into range, and he went down. She yelled, "I'm going after the ones who escaped," then turned toward the doors.

They slammed shut in front of her, and another one of the heavy gates fell to block her path, dropping several inches under the floor's surface into a hidden channel. These bars were so close together that there would be no bending them aside. "Dammit," she muttered and spun back to deal with the bad guys who weren't on the other side of the barrier.

CHAPTER FOUR

Cleaning out the remainder of the enemies took only a few minutes. After their numbers fell below a critical mass, they dropped to their knees and surrendered, and Diana's agents converged to bind their hands and feet with zip ties and stabilize those in need of medical attention. Meanwhile, the rest of them moved to the back of the room. Diana slammed a force blast out at the gate, but it did nothing more than rattle it.

Morrigan asked, "Maybe fire?"

Ruby shook her head. "We don't have the sort of temperature to melt metal without additional chemicals or whatever. We have to either figure out how to raise it or brute force it."

"I am the brute squad," Rath replied and grew to his seven-foot size in the time it took him to reach the gate. He motioned to Idryll, and the shapeshifter did that thing where she made herself stronger, the muscles in her body bulging enough to seem downright unnatural on her humanoid figure. Together, they gripped the bars and tried to lift the barrier, but it wouldn't budge. Rath, his voice much deeper in this form, said, "Something must be blocking it."

Diana nodded. "Makes sense. Deploys by gravity, probably with a latch that holds it in place on each side once it falls past. Wouldn't even have to be a big one. Let's try again, but use telekinesis to help." They summoned their magics and worked together, and while the metal groaned, it steadfastly refused to rise. Diana sighed. "We're not going to let this stop us. Whatever your hardest-hitting magic is, do what you can to build it up." She raised her voice and called, "Croft, get over here."

It took them a moment to organize the plan, then they created a semi-circle around the door and launched all their magics at once. The gate blew back through the doors, hurtling into the room beyond. It slammed into the tail of a heavy truck headed up a ramp on the opposite side. They charged in, throwing magic at the departing vehicle, but nothing hit. Tony Ryan ran over to some equipment set in the wall, and suddenly their comms worked properly again. Diana snapped, "Glam, Deacon, tell me you have them."

Deacon sounded slightly offended. "Of course. Two drones on the vehicles now. Several are on foot, heading cross-country. We're tasking additional drones to them."

"Good work. We're going after the vehicles. Are the drones armed?"

Glam replied, "Non-lethal only."

"Dammit, why?"

"Because we chose the ones with longer range since you're out in the middle of freaking nowhere, and they can't carry both weapon types because of weight and power issues. Plus, you know, it's not *nice* to kill people."

During the conversation, the teams moved toward a pair of vehicles the escapees had left behind, presumably those that would've contained the defenders. Diana ordered, "Jewel, Barb, Cat, Rambo, with me. We're going after the cars. The rest of you clean up the runners." Affirmative replies came as Diana climbed behind the wheel and Ruby took the shotgun position. The truck wasn't as big as a Humvee, but it was larger than any commercial model she'd ridden in. The tires spun, then grabbed as Diana slammed on the accelerator, and they shot out after their targets.

Now that the comms worked again, data flowed to the lenses of her mask. A small window filled with the feed from the drones and overlaid a wireframe map showing the road and their distance from the targets across the rest of one eye. Three vehicles had escaped, and fortunately the path ahead offered no areas where they could veer off for several miles unless they wanted to go off-roading. Diana ordered, "Bring down a drone. Let's see what a stun blast does to the one in front."

Diana piloted the car smoothly, and Ruby imagined the others were watching the drone feed the same as she was. Rath muttered, "Caltrops. Light, and would be good against cars."

Glam replied, "Excellent idea, Rambo. We'll add that into the next drone design."

"And into my flight equipment, I think."

Ruby made a mental note to do the same for her larger drones. The troll was right. Packed properly, they wouldn't take much space or add much weight, especially if she used the correct materials. *I bet Margrave would know the best choices to balance those imperatives. Plus, he'll be totally into using such an old-school weapon in a new tech craft.* That was one of the qualities they shared, the sheer joy of finding innovative uses for already existing things. The drone caught up and launched its attack. The car swerved slightly but didn't otherwise react. Then the back window rolled down, and a fireball slammed into the drone, destroying it. Glam shouted, "Dammit, now I'm angry."

Ruby watched the feed as the second drone swooped in toward the escapees. This time, it looped around the vehicle's front and rammed into the driver's side of the windshield instead of trying anything fancy. The video went dead, the last view a shocked expression on the man's face behind the wheel, but by then they were near enough to see the convoy in the distance. A cloud of sand, dust, and smoke flew up as the truck tumbled off the road, rolling repeatedly. The number of times it flipped ensured that anyone inside would be concussed, at the least, so they could collect them at leisure later. Ruby dismissed it from her thoughts and focused on the other two. "I have a solution for one, but not the other."

Diana nodded. "Then let's hit the one in the back as we go by." Ruby imagined the truck surging forward, but surely that was only in her mind, as the agent was doubtless already pushing the vehicle for all it was worth. Ruby grabbed the EMP from her belt, then rolled down the passenger side window. Behind her, Morrigan said, "You know I have better aim than you do."

Ruby snorted. "Hardly."

Idryll countered, "I've gone on several patrols with her. It's true. She does. I mean, you're average at best, and she's way above average. Almost as good as I am."

Rath giggled and brushed the knives in his vest that he'd retrieved while they worked on blasting the door down. "I can go for the tires."

Ruby sighed and handed the EMP back over her shoulder. "Fine, *Barb*," she emphasized the call sign as she rolled up her window, "but don't miss. We only have one."

Morrigan took it and breathed, "My precious," making everyone on the comms laugh.

Croft's voice broke in to announce that they'd captured the runners and were returning with them to the facility. Diana said, "Make a quick survey of the place and take whatever seems important, in addition to any artifacts they left behind."

Ruby asked, "Why the rush?" She'd figured they would go back and spend some time gathering intelligence.

Diana nodded forward and to the left. "Drone at eleven o'clock, forty degrees up. Not one of ours, I'm guessing."

Glam confirmed, "Nope. I'm bringing the other two toward you, but they won't be in range for another four or five minutes."

Ruby growled, "Damn Paranormal Defense Agency. I'm so tired of those bastards."

Idryll laughed. "Probably not as tired of them as they are of you, though."

"Fair point." The conversation died as they pulled even with the second truck. Morrigan primed the EMP grenade, waited the perfect amount of time, then lobbed it at the other vehicle. Diana swerved off the road, and their progress became a series of bumps and jolts. A loud *crump* sounded as the projectile detonated, and the enemy SUV immediately fell back.

"Bloody hell," Diana snarled. "If they have artifacts in there, they'll be gone with them before we can get there to clean them up."

Rath replied, "On it," and his window whisked down. As he started climbing out, headed for the roof, Idryll followed.

Ruby said, "Be careful."

The shapeshifter laughed. "When am I not?"

Ruby opened her window and stuck her head around, and a moment later saw Rath airborne, his mechanical wings extended as he flew back toward the enemy car. Idryll hit the ground running from her leap, her impressive speed carrying her in the direction of the disabled vehicle.

The ride had smoothed out once Diana rejoined the road, and Ruby climbed onto the roof. Morrigan joined her a moment later. A conveniently placed cargo rack on the top had room for her to shove her boots under it, and she wedged herself in place. Her sister did the same beside her, then hit the button to extend her bow and put an arrow to it. Ruby asked, "Razor?"

Her sister nodded. "Don't think I can risk any of the others."

"Okay. If it doesn't work, I'll hit the thing with the force blast, see if I can break the windows, and force them off the road. I doubt I have the power to knock the car over, but I'll give it a good try."

Diana laughed. "You two are crazy. Perfect to work with us."

Glam said, "Hey, I resemble that remark."

The agents' leader groaned. "Really? You're the brightest bulb on the team, and that's the best line you could come up with? Try harder."

Morrigan's arrow flew true and slammed into the back tire. The car slewed immediately, then tumbled forward along the pavement. Diana hit the brakes to avoid crashing into it, and with a sudden wrench, Ruby was involuntarily airborne. She twisted in midair and sent a fireball at the PDA drone that had closed to watch the conclusion of the chase. She cushioned her landing with a full-body force cocoon a moment before she struck the ground.

Diana sounded amused. "That wasn't nice. No wonder the PDA doesn't like you."

Ruby groaned as she finally stopped rolling, fought down nausea, and let her hands fall to the sides as she stared up into the night. *Not sure if those stars are really there or if they're spinning around my head cartoon style.* She coughed and replied, "He sends drones after me, and I knock them out of the sky. It's a thing we have."

Rath's voice chimed in, "A sign of true love if ever there was one." The rest of the agents echoed his gleeful laughter. Ruby shook her head, realized it hurt, and closed her eyes, checking out of the situation until someone came to get her.

CHAPTER FIVE

Paul Andrews resisted the urge to throw the computer tablet he gripped with white fingers across the room. Despite his outward appearance as a polished professional, complete with a three-piece suit and pocket watch today, he was as furious as he could remember being in the recent past. He forced his voice to remain calm and relaxed the death grip on the tablet, setting it carefully on the table in front of him and clasping his hands behind his back. No one would notice that they clenched into fists as long as he didn't turn around. "So, what you're saying is that we had no information on this major event within our jurisdiction ahead of time, and aside from a single drone, no coverage of it?"

The chamber could be mistaken for a business conference room since that's what it had been in a previous life. They had taken the top floor of an office building in one of the city's industrial parks as theirs. The people seated around him might've been junior executives in their suits, ties, and formal blouses according to preference. They weren't. Instead, they were the sharp tip of the spear that defended Northern Nevada from rogue magicals. *Heaven knows we have plenty of those here.*

His second-in-command Charlotte Krenn nodded, braver than the rest. "That's exactly right, boss. It happened a long way outside the city, and we don't have the sort of surveillance network in place out there as we do here in town."

Her calm, rational tone cut through some of his anger. "So, early information said this looked like a government operation. Do we have any new data?" The event had transpired the previous night, and he'd enjoyed a good night's sleep while his people researched it. Another team member, a man with a five o'clock shadow from his nocturnal work session, replied, "Nothing useful. Black outfits, nothing obvious to tell us who they were. We're enhancing the footage where we can, but as soon as the drone got close enough to see anything clearly, the fireball took it out."

Paul shook his head. "Why aren't those things hardened against magic attacks?"

The chief technical person of his operation, not coincidentally the youngest agent as well, replied, "They are. The blast was sufficiently powerful to break through. Even though our models are bigger than the norm, they're not exactly armor-plated. It's a balancing act between range, armament, and defensive strength."

Andrews cut him off with a raised hand, getting the sense that the man could happily talk for an hour on the subject. "I understand. So, what we need is more of them, then. Surveillance report."

A woman at the far end of the table with short spiky black hair and a muscular physique that strained the seams of her clothes replied, "We have the Strip locked down. We're into the cameras there and have regular drone patrols going. The casinos won't give us access to their feeds, of course." Her derisive tone set off additional grumbles around the room. She continued, "We've rented two apartments south of the Strip and nothing north. We tasked the drones that fly over the main drag to loop through the area between it and the mountains in that direction afterward. The rentals have surveillance outposts and drone installations on the roofs."

He nodded. "When we finish here, let's drop in on them. No warnings," he cautioned. Random inspections were a standard part of his leadership toolkit. "So, what's the limiting factor keeping us from knowing everything there is to know?"

She gave a slight shrug. "Equipment, naturally. We only have so many resources to pull in, and headquarters has been reluctant to give us more." Andrews scowled. Despite taking on the situation in Ely while continuing to maintain an appropriate presence in Reno, he hadn't received much in the way of additional material support from the higher-ups. *They say they reward initiative, but when you actually take some of it, turns out that's just talk.* He set that thought aside for later consideration.

"Okay. I get our limitations. Time to start thinking about how to overcome them. Charlotte and Imera, you're with me. The rest of you, from now until five o'clock, your only job is to figure out ways to get an edge on the chaos in this city, starting with the costumed freaks that keep showing up. I don't know if these mysterious strangers from last night are in league with them or what, but we can't rule it out." He saw flickers of concern on several faces and knew they considered his preoccupation with the magicals who were allegedly defending Magic City overblown. *That's because you didn't have one in your bedroom, detonating your furniture and trying to cut you to shreds with it.* "Let's get it done, people."

From the back seat of one of the unremarkable black SUVs the PDA used, Imera, the one with the spiky hair, asked, "Do you think the locals were involved?"

He shrugged and grunted as he played the surveillance video from the drone on his phone, then snarled in frustration when the feed went away in a blossom of orange fire. "I *feel* it. I think they're way more tapped in than they seem. I mean, it's a great disguise, right? You appear to be an outsider, but you have connections. Like the unnamed government agency. Like the sheriff's office." The last words came out as a snarl. While they'd received nothing but cooperation from the Ely Police Department, Sheriff Alejo and her people were a different story entirely. They hadn't stepped up to join the fight, and while they didn't appear interested in derailing his efforts, either, he couldn't shake the feeling they were acting against him in some manner. *Okay, if you keep it up, you are going to get paranoid. Knock it off.*

The SUV parallel parked itself in front of the apartment building containing their outpost, Charlotte content to let the autonomous function take over for that operation. *Pretty soon, no one's going to know how to drive a stick, and no one will be able to park worth a damn. Computers are great and all, but they're not the solution to everything.* A hint of an idea blossomed deep in his brain at that thought but wouldn't rise to the surface immediately. *Like my father always said, ideas always come out when they're ready, as long as you listen.*

He delayed exiting while his agents got out of the car and checked the area, the standard protocol now so often repeated that it had become unconscious. He liked being in charge, enjoyed the status and small benefits that came with it. Nevada was one more stepping stone, and he expected he'd move up to a bigger location in a couple of years. *Less, maybe, if I can put Magic City to rights. Which I will.*

They took the stairs rather than the elevator, climbing the four stories to the top floor. The buildings they'd chosen both rose higher than those around, giving the drones a less obvious launch point than they would have on a lower structure. The door read the tags in their ID bracelets and opened for them. Inside, the apartment was smallish, with a combination kitchen and dining room, a living room, a single bathroom, and a couple of bedrooms. Three agents lived there, ensuring round-the-clock coverage of the drones' efforts. The other rental space was identical.

They'd pushed furniture that came with the place to the sides, and a wraparound desk holding computer monitors and interface devices sat in a semi-circle with an expensive ergonomic chair in the center. The tech who'd been sitting in it had risen in alarm at their entrance, then remained standing as he approached.

"Agent Crenshaw, how are things?" Paul had checked the roster of people assigned to the apartments on the way over.

The man stammered, "Very good, Director. Our drones are patrolling at just about maximum efficiency, although one is down for repairs outside its usual cycle." A bedroom in each apartment had been converted into a workshop to service the aerial vehicles.

Andrews nodded. "How can we do this better?"

"Pardon me?"

He chuckled at the look of surprise on the other man's face. "You're closest to this operation. How would you make it more efficient, more effective, or ideally both?"

The man shrugged. "More drones. We have the capacity with our AI bots to run an almost unlimited number. We might need some additional server power to review the take, but that's consumer stuff, not hard to come by."

"What if we were in a situation where we didn't have a lot of resources to commit?"

The man signaled for him to walk around the desk and sat in his chair to tap on some controls. "Frankly, what we're using right now is overkill. They're basically fighter drones detailed to normal surveillance. While I'm not saying we should get rid of any of them, we could supplement with prosumer models, tweaked a bit to ensure encrypted communication. Wright and I have been playing with one to judge how well it works."

He hit a button and gestured at the monitor, which showed a docking station on the roof. The image changed as the drone rose and flew toward the Strip. "As you can see, compared to our full function drones, the video feed isn't quite as crisp, and it doesn't move quite as fast. Still, with the affordable price point, we could easily get half again as much surveillance as we're currently running for the cost of one full-fledged fighter drone."

Andrews watched the feed for a moment and decided that the idea had merit. "Very good. Make it happen. Good job." He clapped the man on the shoulder and headed for the door. In the stairwell on the way down, the idea that had sparked earlier surfaced, brought to life by the man's suggestion of additional drones. "Once we get these new drones in play, continue unbroken twenty-four-seven coverage of the Strip, add in the headquarters of the local security companies and the sheriff's office right away, and all the magical shops as our fleet expands. In the meantime, we'll use human intelligence to cover what we don't have the drones for."

Charlotte replied calmly, "We don't have the personnel for that, boss."

He laughed. "That issue is now *your* problem. Get more. I'd start by pulling them in from the Academy and maybe consider reaching out to the Staties for personnel. Call it an internship, pay them a decent wage, play on their loyalty, offer to babysit their pets, whatever you have to do. We're going to lock this damn city down so tight that the instant those vigilantes move, we'll have them dead to rights."

CHAPTER SIX

The motorcycle purred beneath her as Ruby gunned it a little to stay in position in the convoy. It wasn't her wonderful ARCH 1, which some truly evil people with no appreciation for style or aesthetics had destroyed, but a Triumph Roadster she'd borrowed in the meantime. The machine was almost the opposite of her beloved bike: big, heavy, and menacing. It suited her current mood well. She'd spent several hours meditating to lock up the artifact in her arm before joining the Desert Ghosts for their weekly supply run. It felt great to be out and about, the Mist Elf disguise that wasn't quite her granting a sense of anonymity. She didn't have her sword with her, but she'd concealed her gun in a shoulder holster under her light leather jacket, and a dagger rode at her waist. She was hypervigilant for trouble, but none seemed to be in the offing on this sunny day afternoon.

Prex, the dwarven leader of the club, spoke into the radio that only the two of them shared. "Enjoying yourself?"

Ruby replied, "Totally." It was always fantastic to see what businesses and individuals were willing to donate for the good of their community. All of it wound up at the abbey on the hill, and she presumed from there it was distributed to folks in need or stored against future requirements. She didn't trust many people, but both the head of the Desert Ghosts and the abbey's Abbot numbered among them. A PDA drone zoomed by overhead, and she flipped it off.

The dwarf laughed. "Not a fan, huh?"

"Definitely not. Those guys are jerks. So, what do you know?" Information-sharing was an established part of their relationship, and he understood she would often be able to share less than he would. He seemed fine with the uneven arrangement. "There's a lot of buzz on the street about a Drow dude. He's apparently fighting back against human overreach."

Ruby forced her face to stay neutral. She'd met the Dark Elf, and they didn't see eye to eye on any number of issues, "human overreach" prominent among them. She replied, "How do you feel about that?"

Prex laughed again. "I can tell from your tone you're not a believer. I'm not really, either, but I do think there's been a disproportionate amount of ownership taken by humans in what is fundamentally a magical city. Hell, it's right there in the name."

Ruby admired the man's ability to discuss touchy subjects without losing his sense of humor. She'd never seen him angry but imagined it would probably be a frightful sight, based on nothing beyond a gut feeling. "I get that there are some humans who aren't being properly respectful of others. That may be related to species, or it might just be people being scumbags. I think you could say that of some magicals, too. It seems to me he's painting with a little too broad a brush."

"I don't know. Could be a need for it at this point. You have to admit, humans are all over the place now, with their police patrols and their ubiquitous drones."

Ruby made a "wooo" sound. "Ubiquitous is a pretty big word for a biker gang member."

"Screw you," he said genially. "Come on, be honest. You don't like it either."

A few moments passed as she gave the question the consideration it deserved. With a shake of her head, she replied, "I'll admit to thinking some of the complaints might be valid. But, again, wanton violence is probably not the answer."

He laughed. "More like carefully directed violence, right?"

She grinned. "Now you're speaking my language. Seriously, the Paranoid Defense Agency doesn't represent humanity very well."

"Those bastards. Here's a piece of information you might not have. I'm pretty sure those government slimeballs have co-opted the self-driving cars that carry tourists around town."

"What?"

He sounded satisfied to have surprised her. "Yep. We had the opportunity to, uh, get a solid look inside one of them recently." Ruby knew the gang occasionally did things that strayed across the line separating legal from illegal, but property crime wasn't her concern. *Except on a large scale, like casinos collapsing.* He continued, "We discovered an encrypted transmitter hooked into the vehicle's computer system. Our resident techie said that with the right software, it could be pulling information from the cameras the car uses for its AI driving. I doubt it can get anything from the magical component, but between the cameras, data on the occupants, and the vehicles' constant presence throughout the city, it's a gold mine of information."

Ruby frowned. "Well, that sucks hard."

"Exactly. So, sure, a lot of humans are okay, but some of them are right bastards."

Thinking of Agent Paul Andrews and the trap he'd tried to set for her, she replied, "True that, brother."

She threaded a little magic into her body to assist with carrying the heavy box up to the abbey and felt comfortable and refreshed when they arrived. They had the transfer down to a science, and a steady line of abbey brothers came out to take the loads off their hands. The gang members headed inside to the brewing area, where they'd sit at the long table that dominated the center of it all and enjoy a pint before heading home. On a previous visit, Abbott Thomas had confided that on some occasions it was more than a single pint, and no one was allowed back to their bikes until they'd slept it off or magicked the inebriation away, depending on their preference. The long white-haired and short white-bearded and mustached head of the Abbey smiled as she surrendered her burden and entered the brew hall. His robe looked like the same beat-up one he'd worn every time they'd interacted. "Ruby, so good to see you."

She matched his expression. "Abbott Thomas, you, too."

"I have a special batch for you to try if you're interested." They had bonded over a love of craft beer, although Ruby's passion for it didn't approach his level. She nodded. "Only an idiot would turn down such an offer. Despite the opinion that my sister and my friend Idryll share, I am not *that* stupid."

He laughed and gestured her toward a small room at the back of the chamber. As they walked, he asked, "How are they? Is your sister fully recovered?"

"She seems to be." Morrigan's kidnapping had caused less surface-level anxiety than Ruby would've expected, and she wondered if she had truly dealt with the experience or had merely buried it for a while. Ruby had tried the latter tactic on any number of occasions and knew that if she had, the issue would come back up eventually, and probably at an inconvenient moment.

Thomas nodded. "Excellent." He opened the door and led her into the modest chamber. A smallish brewing setup occupied the left-hand part of the room, and a square table, about three feet on a side, with a trio of chairs around it, was pushed against the opposite wall. She lowered herself into a seat while he drew two mugs of beer. He handed her one, sat at an angle, and raised his glass. She clinked it with hers, and he offered, "To peace and harmony."

She finished the toast as she always did with him. "Through the liberal application of alcohol." He laughed, and they both drank. The flavors on her tongue were fantastic, and as usual, mostly impenetrable. She thought she had identified one, though. "Honey?"

He nodded. "Very good. We'll make a brewer out of you yet."

A raucous set of noises came from the other room, and he rose to investigate. She did the same and looked over his shoulder to see a human family sitting amongst the Desert Ghosts, a middle-aged man and woman and two kids—a boy and a girl—both below ten. Ruby commented, "The perfect nuclear family. Who are they?"

He shut the door, and they returned to the table. "The Kincaids. Their house burned down recently, and they're staying with us until they get things figured out."

"It's a good thing you do here, helping people who've had random events smash into and up-end their lives."

He took a deep drink and set the mug down with a sigh, then lifted his eyes to meet hers. "Interesting choice of adjective, there. 'Random.' Indications are that the house was deliberately set aflame."

Ruby frowned. "I haven't heard anything about that."

Abbott Thomas shrugged. "I have contacts in the fire department. They're not officially calling it arson because they can't find an accelerant, but it appears to have burned way hotter than it should have."

She set her mug carefully down on the table. "You're suggesting magic."

"I am."

"Any other reason to think that was the cause?"

He shrugged. "None that I know of. I did make inquiries with the Ely Police Department, but they're reluctant to share information of late."

She growled, "With the PDA watching over their shoulder, I'm not surprised. Did you reach out to Sheriff Alejo?"

He shook his head. "I don't have the sort of relationship with the sheriff that would allow me to ask that delicate question."

"I do, and I will." She changed the subject. "Is there anything you need for this place? I mean, not for the people you help, but for you all?"

He laughed. "We're pretty self-sufficient. But, you know, if you happen to come across any interesting flavors or unique plants in your travels, I'd love to have them. New varieties require lots of experimentation." He rose and refilled their mugs, then sat again. "And intensive testing. For instance, is this one of those brews where the second mug goes down as well as the first? Only one way to find out."

Ruby laughed. "Now that's a task I'm definitely willing to take on." *First, magical items for Shentia and books for the mystics. Now, components for beer making. Pretty soon I'm going to be nothing but a wandering scavenger.* She thought about that for a second, then grinned. *Actually, doesn't sound like such a bad gig. Also, that's totally my band name if I ever have one.*

CHAPTER SEVEN

Ruby had planned to drop in on Sheriff Alejo at her office, but Demetrius's bots in charge of monitoring the police scanner channels set her in a different direction. She made her way to the city's southwest corner, to a factory that had been a fixture in the area for more than half a century. It was a fixture no more, however. The main building was ablaze, sending smoke billowing into the sky. Explosions repeatedly *cracked* in an irregular beat, and police and firefighters kept their distance more than actively seeking to stop the blaze. The strategy was entirely logical since the other buildings were far enough away that they probably wouldn't catch, and the conflagration was too intense for them to have any chance of saving the structure.

She called Alejo's cell phone from her untraceable comm, and when the sheriff picked up, said, "Time for a chat? Go around the corner of the building behind you."

Alejo didn't reply, merely shoved the phone in her pocket and turned with a scowl visible despite the distance that separated them. Ruby crossed the roof, jumped down, and greeted the sheriff as she came into view. "That's a doozy."

Valentina Alejo nodded. "Firefighters say it's the worst they've ever seen. I guess that's what happens when you light up a plastics factory. Casinos are going to be scrambling to find new vendors." The other woman shook her head, looking irritated at the situation. "Something I can do for you?"

The words emerged in her professional, brusque tone, but Ruby took no offense. It was simply the sheriff in sheriff mode. "I wanted to check in and see if the PDA has been causing you any trouble. Some people I trust who work on the Strip say their presence has expanded dramatically."

Alejo shook her head. "I haven't seen any evidence of that, but admittedly I'm not watching the main part of the city since that's Ely PD jurisdiction."

"Did they reach out to you?"

The sheriff shrugged. "A while ago, as you know. Lately, no. I'm keeping an eye on them, all the same."

"You'd think that people on the same side shouldn't have to do that."

The other woman barked a laugh. "I wouldn't assume we're on the same side. First, they're federal. Second, a scumbag leads them."

"I can't argue with that. Anyway, I also wanted to make you aware that some of my friends believe the PDA is using autonomous cars for surveillance throughout the city."

Alejo scowled. "That would break all sorts of laws, I would think. Unless, of course, the government helped fund the companies and wrote themselves in some special privileges." She sighed. "That's the trouble with this secretive spy stuff. Too many unknowns."

A large *crash* sounded from the factory, and they peered around the corner to find that the roof had caved in entirely. Ruby shook her head. "Seems like fires are popping up all over lately. Maybe it's the heat. I met a family earlier today whose house burned down. The Kincaids."

Alejo grunted. "I have one of them in lockup right now."

"What?"

"Yeah, oldest child, a son, seventeen going on stupid. He wound up in a drunken fight outside a bar. He shouldn't have been in there anyway, but fake IDs aren't too hard to come by in this new magical age."

Suspicion bloomed inside Ruby. "Who was involved?"

"A bunch of drunk idiot humans against a bunch of drunk idiot dwarves. No one we took in could explain why they were fighting, only that they were. The dwarves didn't use magic but still put several of the humans in the hospital and were the unquestioned winner of the fracas."

A chill ran down her spine. *There's no way that's a coincidence.* "You might want to keep an eye on the other non-magicals involved for a while."

Alejo's frown intensified. "What do you know?"

Ruby shook her head. "Nothing specific. Only a hunch. It's probably worth taking a second look at any situation where magicals and humans are battling though."

The other woman let out a frustrated sigh. "I'm aware you're the secretive type, but now's not the time to hold anything back."

Ruby lifted an eyebrow. "Is there ever a time for that, in your eyes?"

A short laugh escaped Alejo. "Well, no, but that's not the point. Give me whatever you can, whenever you can, and I'll do the same."

She nodded. "Our agreement holds. Whatever I can share, I will share. Speaking of which, what do you hear about the investigation into the collapse of the Mist?"

Alejo hooked her thumbs into her weapons belt. "Nothing new. The investigators hung it all on Sloane, who is conveniently dead, which allowed them to close the book on it. Now it's just wrapping up details and running the process."

Ruby growled, "Dammit. That's too easy."

"And nothing's easy in Magic City."

"Exactly what I was thinking. Sloane didn't do it alone, and the masked man and the fancy soldier he had with him wouldn't have been enough to accomplish all that. There *must* be more players on the field that we don't see yet."

Alejo shrugged. "As long as no one's bringing down any more casinos, do we really care?"

Ruby nodded. "I care. They're a threat until we identify and remove them."

"Speaking of difficulty identifying things, I hear tell of a local trafficking ring in magic items getting busted by some government agency. Standard special ops, black uniforms with no markings, masks and helmet kind of deal. Know anything about that?"

Ruby snorted softly. "I might have heard a thing or two. Nothing I can share, though."

"Was it at least a successful bust?"

"If I had any insight into such an event, which I'm not saying I do, I'd say that the operation met its objectives to disrupt the trafficking and shut down a certain compound utilized as a base."

"Compound?" Ruby had used the word by choice, intending to offer the sheriff a clue about where she might investigate. "Interesting. Anyway, just you remember, and feel free to share this with anyone who needs to hear it. There's a line in my jurisdiction, even for out-of-towners. Everyone should be careful not to cross it, or all cooperation goes out the window." Alejo's eyes stared directly into Ruby's lenses.

"Always. It's front of mind, trust me. Anyway, last piece of info, I'm going to be away for a bit. I have a thing to do out of town. Stay safe."

Alejo nodded, already turning back toward the accident scene as she replied, "You too, masked stranger."

Ruby laughed as she watched the other woman depart. *You're good people, Alejo. But believe me, you don't want to look too deeply at Diana and her friends.* She thought about that for a second, then reconsidered. *Actually, I wonder how you'd fit in with her and her team.* She considered it a little further and laughed again. *Nah, you're not nearly crazy enough to be part of that bunch.*

CHAPTER EIGHT

Morrigan moved from rooftop to rooftop through the southern part of Ely, forcing her distracted mind to concentrate only on the next step, on maintaining her silence and concealment. She'd chosen to patrol alone, leaving the house at midday to nap in her office at Spirits to avoid any complications with Ruby or Idryll. Since her kidnapping, since she'd been indescribably stupid enough to let the enemy get the drop on her, sleep came haphazardly. Motion was better. There was a purity in the exercise of her body and brain with a purpose.

She was well aware that any competent therapist would point out that her current mental state wasn't completely normal. She was suffused with anger and figured pushing that energy outward against anyone who might cause trouble in Magic City was better than focusing it inward and rehashing past mistakes. *Like Margrave says, every mistake is valuable as long as you learn from it and don't die.*

She'd spent a good part of the sleepless portion of the night before crafting and sharpening new razor arrows.

Now each slot in her quiver held some sort of offensive capability. Adding more potentially lethal choices ran the risk of running afoul of Alejo's mandate not to drop bodies, but Morrigan was utterly confident in her ability to shoot to wound. *If there's a doubt, I'll use something different.*

She'd decided the best way to figure out what the Drow was up to was to follow humans who might be likely targets—those acting like idiots. If there were groups of magicals out looking to cause trouble, they would doubtless be doing the same thing. So, she headed to the club that was the lowest-hanging fruit, where the drinks were cheap, and the tourists who ventured off the Strip tended to congregate and pregame before going out for their serious carousing. The front was glass block and neon. The door was painted red with a strange moon-shaped window cut into it. She'd never been inside the bar but had heard stories galore, and they were sufficient to ensure she never wanted to cross the threshold. *If "Eww" was a location, that'd be it.*

It was only a matter of waiting ten minutes before a group of rowdy boys—*well, men, I guess*—left the establishment. Margrave had converted the listening device he'd made for Ruby into one small enough to attach to her wrist, and she pointed it at them. Their words filtered into the connected earpiece. "All right, let's find a good place to get our drink on." A second voice replied, "And some girls, cute ones this time."

Another group member laughed and added, "But not too smart, and a little on the wild side." Morrigan rolled her eyes. *I seem to have found the idiots I was looking for. Not sure if they're trying to live the college dream they saw in the movies or if that's how they really are. Either way, they're going to get themselves in trouble due to their stupidity. I can't let them be bait. Too dangerous.*

Her original plan fell away as another replaced it, inspiring a grin. She paralleled their movement, and when they stepped into an alleyway, saw her chance. She focused her mind and her magic, imagining human versions of Jessica Rabbit if she was a sorority girl. An illusory trio of women walked past the mouth of the alley in full view of the boys. *No, men, even if they act like boys.* She'd made them all top-heavy, all blonde, and all dressed in tight club clothes.

The men called after them and increased their speed, and she had one of the illusions wave before moving out of sight. She rushed to the opposite side of the roof in time to solidify them again so that the men would spot them half a block away as they came around the corner. She gave the women a little more sashay in their step and laughed as a man stumbled, his eyes not properly on where he was going. *Distracted, much? Seriously, there should be some sort of hormone depressant pill you guys take until your brains catch up with your bodies.*

One of the boys called, "Hey, wait up," and with a soft laugh, Morrigan ventriloquized through her illusion, "Oh, come on, guys. Surely you can catch us." She had the blondes increase their speed, and the men ran after them. Her magic led the frat boys, which is how she'd come to think of them, on a merry chase, their quarry always half a block ahead, disappearing around the corner before they could reach them. Finally, she had the figures vanish in the entryway of a fairly reputable club closer to the Strip, where the pursuing group would probably be safe. To their credit, they had all remained good-natured about the pursuit, not developing into nasty comments or the sort of talk that might have ticked her off. She was laughing as she left them behind and headed further south.

Her mirth vanished as she spotted a trio of magicals in an alley. They registered to her eyes as suspicious right off the bat, and when they stopped at the back entrance of a store, she knew she'd found someone at least interested in breaking the law. *That doesn't mean they're working for the Drow, of course.* She called up a map on her secure phone and researched the business, finding it was a human-owned jewelry store specializing in estate sale items and antiques. Not big money because the big-money jewelry stores were in the casinos, but they would still have a fairly valuable inventory. It wasn't conclusive, but she was in the mood to mix it up, so it would do.

She pulled a grapple attached to a thin cord from her belt and secured it to the edge of the roof, then lowered herself silently into the alley, hidden by the building's shadows. She could've used her magic, but she didn't want to make that loud an entrance. When she reached the bottom, she tapped the control that wirelessly instructed the grapple to retract its claws, and the line re-spooled with a whisper. She drew her collapsed bow from its left thigh holster and pressed the button to extend it, reaching back for her lightning stun arrow. She nocked and loosed it as soon as the bow constructed, taking out the member of the group who was separated from the others, watching the far end of the alley. It struck true, and he jittered and danced before collapsing. The other two, who had been working on the door, straightened and turned in her direction. She considered shooting them with arrows or anti-magic rounds from the pistol in the drop holster on her right leg, but discarded those ideas. *Nah, let's do it the old-fashioned way.* She collapsed the bow and charged toward them.

They stepped away from each other, one to each side of the alley, and sent fireballs at her. She used magic to propel herself up and over them, wrapping herself in a force cocoon in midair. Their power covered her as she landed, but when the flames faded, she was unscathed. She let the shields fall. "Come on, boys, surely you don't need to use fancy powers on little old me."

She started toward the one on the right and led with a slow right hook. He smiled condescendingly and lifted his arm to block, then twisted and drove his other fist at her stomach. Now that they were engaged, his partner couldn't use his magic, and she felt him circle behind her instead. *Oh no, none of that.* She whipped the right hand he had blocked and held up high down in a C-shape to slam a hammer fist into his ribs as she stopped the other. She felt the satisfying crunch as at least one bone gave way under the impact. The air *whooshed* out of him, and she raised his captive hand and spun underneath it, twisting his arm. With a solid yank, she could've given him a spiral fracture from wrist to shoulder but didn't see the need to do quite that much damage. Instead, she used the limb to propel him at his partner, who danced nimbly out of the way.

Morrigan taunted, "He's slow. I hope you're faster."

The elf replied, "Once we finish beating you down,

that's only the beginning of your pain, little girl." He strode ahead menacingly.

She sighed. "You know, I was going to give you the benefit of the doubt. When you say things like that, you come off as someone who shouldn't be allowed near women. So, Plan B." She skipped forward and punched both fists at his throat, forcing him to block down with both arms and leaving his head undefended. She snapped her forehead into his nose, which crunched under the impact. He stepped backward, his hands automatically rising to cover the damaged area.

The other one slipped in again, slower but still in the fight. He'd produced a knife from somewhere, a small switchblade that thoroughly failed to impress her. He skipped in and stabbed at her, and she caught it in an X-block with her wrists, then grabbed his wrist and yanked it in a direction it wasn't supposed to go. The joint snapped, the blade fell to the ground, and she finished with a side-kick to his sternum that sent him gasping to the pavement.

Broken nose advanced with murder in his eyes, and she shook her head. "It's been fun, but I have to go. Sorry fellas." He threw a series of jabs that she intercepted, then opened himself up when he thought he had a window to land a wicked offhand hook. She blocked it and skipped forward, ramming a knee up into his groin. He fell to the ground, whimpering. "Maybe think about *that* the next time you threaten a woman that way."

A scuff from behind threw her into an automatic response. She spun and drew her pistol, summoning a force shield to protect herself. The trigger was halfway depressed before she realized it was another of the bad guys and that he was far enough away that she could easily defend against him. She yanked the barrel downward, and the bullet that would've taken him in the center of his chest caught him in the leg instead. He twisted and fell to the ground with a scream.

Morrigan remained locked in place, hyperventilating momentarily, then holstered the weapon and knelt beside him. "You're an *idiot*. Do you realize how close you were to dying?" She popped the cap on one of her healing potions and poured it between his lips. *Do* you *realize how close* you *were to breaking the rules because you panicked?*

Morrigan growled and told her inner voice to shut up. A carefully calculated application of force magic *thumped* their heads against the ground to knock them out, then she blasted herself up to the roof and called the police department to clean up the magicals. Chances were good that someone was already en route given all the cameras around. *Tense times for everyone in Magic City, apparently, including me. Maybe I should stop by and chat with Challen about my mental state sooner rather than later.*

CHAPTER NINE

Ruby crossed the threshold from one world to the other, letting the portal close behind her in the living room of her family's home on Oriceran. She wandered into what had been her bedroom and was now her dressing chamber. She'd changed the space over time, moving this or that item on each visit until it suited her current needs. Idryll shifted into cat form and made herself comfortable on a nearby pillow.

The heavy wardrobe creaked as she opened it, and she ran her fingers over the old, polished wood. It was always strange coming to this place, so unlike the technological world she spent most of her time in. She stripped out of her jeans and T-shirt, folded them carefully and set them aside, then pulled on the base layer of thin but strong leather Keshalla had acquired for her. The brilliant blue and silver portions offset the black beautifully. She took a moment to regard herself in the mirror, covered wrist to ankle and up to her neck in the tight sheath. It reminded her who she was on Oriceran, helped her focus on the importance of the events to come.

I wonder how many people reached this far in the process and what became of those who went no further. The mystics had records of another Mirra from before Kaeni but had lost any others to time. She had originally figured there would be one per generation, but in fact, it seemed like there were less than that, at least from what Nadar and the archivist had shared.

She fastened the tooled leather belt and slipped her daggers into the attached sheaths, then pulled her boots with their hidden throwing knives back on again. Her sword went into a new scabbard, left behind with a note by Keshalla. It looped diagonally over her chest, the strap connecting to the belt to hold the whole thing in place. The designs on it matched the ones on her belt, and the material was identical.

When she finished, she felt extremely underdressed, compared to the amount of gear she normally carried on the other planet. However, she did feel faster and more nimble without the weight of the vest and other stuff. *Speed will probably serve me best since I have no idea what's coming.*

She pulled her hair back in a ponytail and tied it with two beaded holders that trailed down to the middle of her shoulders. She whipped her head around in each direction, noting that the beads fell just short of reaching anything vital. *Perfect.* The final touch was slipping healing and energy potions into her thigh pouches. With a deep breath, she dropped into the lotus position and reached a hand over her shoulder to grip the hilt of her sword. She landed in the construct she'd created for conversation with Shalia and Tyrsh, comfortable chairs on an ornate rug in the center of an expansive grassland. A warm breeze caressed her skin as the entities inside her sword greeted her.

Shalia said, "It's good to see you again."

She nodded. "You as well."

The other personality, generally more confrontational, added, "Perhaps you should visit more often."

Ruby chuckled. "Even if I used you in each battle and trained with you for hours every day, it still wouldn't be enough to satisfy your need for attention."

His sister entity laughed, and he grudgingly chuckled as well. Shalia asked, "Why now?"

She replied, "I'm about to embark on the third *venamisha*."

Both of their mouths formed identical "Os" in response. Tyrsh said, "We are aware of only one other who has done so, *Mirra* Kaeni."

"And before her, *Mirra* Mintel. Those are the only two I'm aware of. You'd think there'd be more, though."

Shalia shrugged. "Since we don't know what the test entails, we cannot reasonably draw such a conclusion. For all we know, it requires the utmost luck to survive."

Ruby rolled her eyes. "You know, that's not exactly the sort of reassurance I hoped for." The others laughed, and she continued, "I welcome your counsel as we go along. But, please give it judiciously. I have the sense that a slip of any kind, a distraction at the wrong moment, for instance, would spell doom."

They both adopted identical sober expressions. "You

have our commitment," the female said. The male finished, "That we will do our utmost to assist and not to hinder."

Ruby nodded. "More than that, I cannot ask." She released the hilt and rose to her feet with a slow spin, cracking her neck and stretching out her arms. "Let's get a move on, kitty cat." She shook out her hands before opening the door, padding through her home, and stepping out into the village, followed by Idryll.

The sight that greeted her took her entirely by surprise. It seemed as if every individual who lived there had turned out, and they had formed two lines leading from her home to the centermost boulder in the clearing, leaving a gap barely wide enough for her to walk through. At the far end, her teacher and mentor stood atop the rock, arms crossed, gazing placidly toward her. Ruby felt a smile bloom on her face and stepped forward, gaining confidence with each stride. The villagers extended their hands to touch her, men and women, young and old. They said her name, or her family name, or simply wished her good luck. The overall sense was one of possessiveness, though, as if they affirmed that she belonged to them, and by extension, they to her. Tears dampened her eyes when she arrived next to the boulder and looked up at Keshalla. "This is something. Is it your doing?"

The other woman shook her head. "Word tends to spread regardless of how secret you try to keep things. They must've had someone watching that sensed your arrival at the same moment I did. This is clearly an important occasion for them."

Ruby lifted an eyebrow. "But not for you?"

Her teacher chuckled. "It might be important for me, as well. But only a little." The other woman jumped down from the boulder, and they shared a hug. "Are you ready? You look ready."

Ruby nodded. "Let's get to it. Let me guess, down into the mountain we go."

Keshalla, who had taken the task of researching the next part of the *venamisha* upon herself, replied, "No, actually. The archivist found a journal from *Mirra* Kaeni's time, and the last sight the author had of her before her return was on the way to the top of the mountain."

Ruby groaned. "Probably they want to tire our legs out first. Climb the whole way, *then* have to go down the mountain."

Idryll observed, "You're really whiny about the mountain, you know that? Maybe try to be more, I don't know, adult?"

Her teacher laughed. "Well, at least we'll get to stop and have a snack and a chat with Nadar."

Ruby nodded. "Have you been to the top?"

Keshalla shook her head. "To my knowledge, no one has. It's prohibited, and a magical barrier prevents going beyond a certain point, or so Nadar says."

"That's not ominous at all. Shall we go?"

Their arrival at the mystics' home brought all of them out, as well. They didn't touch her, only nodded respectfully. Nadar ushered them inside and sat them on the familiar couches. Idryll said, "So, wise mystics, do you have clues or secrets to share?" She made a suspicious face, somewhere between distrustful and hopeful, and drew a laugh from everyone in the room.

Nadar, his long dark hair pulled up into a bun, replied, "Not exactly. We do have something for you though. The archivist will be here before too long." They sipped tea, ate trail bread, and talked about innocuous things until the head of the archive, who looked older than she acted, arrived. She bustled forward and sat between Ruby and Idryll, forcing them each to move aside. In her hands was a thick tome with a heavy cover. She opened it to a marked section and handed it over to Ruby. "I think you'll find this interesting."

Ruby scanned the page and found a description of Kaeni's ascent. It included a mention of the barrier being capable of reading the intents of anyone who tried to pass it, and only those with minds properly touched by previous *venamishas* would be able to penetrate it. Ruby read that part out loud, and Idryll snorted. "Oh, I'd say your mind is plenty touched."

Ruby scowled. "You know, you can go home."

"Then you die, and I have to go through a day or two of feeling guilty about that. I don't need that kind of aggravation."

She whipped out a hand and tapped her companion in the ribs, knowing full well that Idryll's greater speed could've stopped her easily. The assemblage laughed at their antics, and the archivist asked, "Do you have all you need?"

Ruby nodded and handed the large volume back over.

The wizened woman reminded her, "If you find any books that look interesting, you'll bring them back for me, right?"

She smiled at the older woman. "Of course."

"Promise?"

Ruby smothered a grin. "Promise." She saw that Idryll and Keshalla were both exerting the same extra control over their expressions and rose. "No time like the present."

Many of the mystics followed as they climbed, but they fell off as the trail wound higher. By the time the trio reached the shimmering barrier, they were alone. Set into the path before the protective shield was a flat, circular stone, large enough for all three of them to stand on, with similar markings to the one she'd seen in the cave during the first *venamisha*. She focused her mind on that experience, and the events of the second, including meeting *Mirra* Kaeni, and stepped onto it after grabbing each of her companions' hands in hers.

Nothing visibly changed, but she sensed something was different. She walked forward as if the barrier didn't exist, and to them, it suddenly didn't. Her eyes blurred a little as they crossed the boundary, then her mouth dropped open at the sight of what awaited them. The trail wound for another quarter mile or so, ending at a huge castle. It was positioned right at the pinnacle and looked ominous and violent, with sharp towers and harshly edged walls, black stone against a swiftly darkening sky. Only then did she realize they had moved from daytime to night in an instant.

Idryll observed, "That place doesn't look at all welcoming."

Keshalla responded with a single laugh. "Guessing we

need to go inside. Is that what your instincts are telling you?"

Ruby nodded. "Got it in one. Here goes nothing."

CHAPTER TEN

Two heavy wooden doors with black metal bands guarded the entrance, but they parted at their approach as if inviting them in to their doom. Crossing that threshold instead of running away to safety took an act of will. Beyond lay a vast room, several stories high, with mammoth chandeliers hanging from a towering, pointed ceiling. They glowed dimly, presumably magically, since she couldn't see any other way for them to function for so long. *Assuming time is a thing here. Maybe I shouldn't count on anything.* A pair of curved staircases led up to a second-floor balcony with a doorway leading beyond. Opposite the entry on the ground level, underneath that balcony, was a second egress.

Another carved circle that covered most of the floor dominated the space. It held four double-life-size statues of people, with room for at least a dozen more before the circumference would be complete. The figures faced inward, and one of them was recognizable. Ruby crept cautiously forward, keeping her senses open for traps or magic. Idryll and Keshalla walked a pace behind to her left and right, respectively. "It's Kaeni." The statue was so smooth that it almost seemed as if it would come to life. The exquisitely rendered folds of her dress looked like real fabric suddenly trapped in time and stripped of color. Among all the grey and black stone, the statues were a glimmering white. "Think it's marble?"

Keshalla confirmed, "Probably is. Oriceran marble, obviously." The version found on Earth wasn't as pure to the eye.

Idryll asked, "Were they all *Mirra*?"

Ruby nodded. "It would make sense. The one before Kaeni was male, as is the statue next to her. Plus, the clothes look like they're from the right era." Another male was beside him, and the first in line was a woman, dressed in an outfit entirely unrecognizable to anything Ruby had seen people wear. They almost looked like hunting leathers, the subtly patterned skin of some long-dead beast. She shook her head. "Well, I feel confident saying that we're in the right place, anyway."

Keshalla observed, "They have one thing in common." She pointed, and Ruby noticed for the first time the thin circlet that sat atop each of their heads, like a daywear crown of Earth's royalty.

I guess that's all the evidence we need. She turned to the others and drew a deep breath. "Okay, probably whatever lies beyond those doorways is the start of the test. Any guesses as to what we'll face this time? Preliminary thoughts?"

Keshalla looked as if she would answer, then donned a slightly confused expression and tilted her head to the side.

"Honestly, I couldn't even hazard a guess. I have the strongest sense that my presence here is simply as an observer. You probably shouldn't count on my help."

Ruby frowned. "You? Backing down from a challenge? Unheard of."

Her mentor laughed. "Oh, I'll try to assist you, believe me. Something tells me the test will prevent me from intervening."

Idryll clapped her hands together. "Fortunately, I don't feel anything like that. I'm ready to see what's through door number one."

Ruby smiled at her. "Together we can handle whatever they can throw at us." She touched the hilts of her knives and reached back to check the draw of her sword, which was perfect as always. Then she squared her shoulders to the exit and walked toward it, the others at her sides. As soon as they stepped into the archway, a heavy portcullis slammed into the ground behind them, and Keshalla vanished. Ruby spun, her daggers instantly filling her hands, but there was no other threat.

She called, "Keshalla?" Only echoes returned. "I guess she was right." She led the way forward into another room, about half the size of the one they'd left and a story lower. Ahead, in the center of the space, sat a pile of heavy rocks, each looking remarkably similar to the boulders in the village clearing. *That makes sense. We're in the same region, and the stones are logically from the same source.*

From behind and above, her mentor's voice announced, "I seem to be stuck up here." They turned to see Keshalla standing with her hands on the railing of the low fence that guarded the balcony one floor up. No staircase led down from it, and she presumed her teacher had already tried to descend by other means.

She called, "Sure, enjoy the show, maybe focus on remembering it so you can write it down for the archivist."

Idryll stage-whispered, "Keshalla's old. She probably can't hold that much in her mind."

A cross-sounding, "Come up here and say that, kitty cat," filtered down from above. Ruby was already pacing toward the center of the room. Her next step forward brought the boulders to life. They began to shift back and forth, and she traded her right-hand dagger for her sword and stepped back defensively. Idryll extended her claws and moved far enough away so that a single attack wouldn't catch them both, even if it were a giant boulder hurtling through the air. The motion intensified, then suddenly the stones started to roll, creating a circle of fast-moving rock.

They completed three rotations, gathering speed before the pattern changed. As if by unseen signal, they all moved simultaneously toward the center of the ring they had created and piled on top of one another. When the rumbling and scraping stopped, a fifteen-foot-high humanoid shape stood before them. It had boulders for feet, boulders for legs, boulders for everything. A face emerged from the top one, seeming to push out from within, and it gave a nod that she would've called respectful in any other circumstance. Its voice grated, sounding remarkably similar to the sound the stones had made as they'd crashed together to assemble him. "Greetings from *Mirra* Inshala. We welcome the *junra* to the third mystery."

Ruby frowned. "You mean the *venamisha?*"

The stone creature nodded. "The words come from the same source and mean almost the same thing. Has that knowledge been lost?"

Idryll replied, "Seems like."

He shook his head. "With each new arrival to the castle, it appears as if your race has forgotten more and more of your history."

Ruby asked, "Who are you?"

"The guardian of this place."

"The castle?"

Boulders ground against each other, making an uncomfortable sound as he shrugged. "This part of it."

Implying there are other parts, potentially with their guardians. Awesome. "Do you have a riddle for me or something?"

"Nothing so innocent. It is my task to prevent you from continuing."

"No other options than fighting, I presume?"

He shook his head again. "No. Only through my destruction will you be permitted to move ahead. Of course, if you wish to leave, to abandon the quest you have undertaken, you have only to say so."

"Did the others go through this?"

"Yes."

Idryll frowned. "Why are you still here, then?"

The creature smiled. "The magic of this place brings me back to resume my watch when the Mist Elves lack a *Mirra.*"

Keshalla called, "How many times have you lost?"

"Four."

Ruby added, "How many times have you won?"

He answered without pride, a simple statement of fact that was nonetheless chilling. "Countless."

"Might as well get on with it, then."

His face vanished, becoming flat stone again, and his body wrenched itself in a fast circle. At the end of it, a boulder flew at both her and Idryll. She shouted, "Let's see if we can hurt him." Having expected an attack of that kind, she easily dropped and rolled out of the way of the projectile and sheathed her sword, deciding to try magic first.

She called up a force shield in her left hand and added the layer around her skin, then threw a force blast at him. It smashed into his torso with no apparent effect. She followed it with frost, thinking that might work against him. *Water overcomes stone eventually, right?* It, too, failed miserably. She stopped her attacks and closed the distance with him as Idryll made a fast pass, her claws scraping against one of his legs and shooting out sparks. No visible sign of her effort was left behind, though. Ruby shouted, "At this rate, we'll have discovered all the things that won't hurt him in a year or two."

Her partner countered sarcastically, "Maybe you should come up with some sort of new idea then, *junra*."

Ruby tried shadow and fire to no avail while dodging more thrown boulders. The assault stopped for a moment, and she had to dive out of the way as the projectiles he'd used returned to his body, and he started tossing them out again. She growled, "Okay, that's enough of that." When a missed projectile came to rest, she used a force blast to knock it back against the wall and wrapped a barrier of the same magic around it to keep it from moving. She'd had abundant practice bisecting her mind to be able to fight while still maintaining the magical fence. Not for the first time, she wondered if all the trials and tribulations she'd experienced recently were tied together in some sort of fate or destiny.

She dropped to her face as another rock whipped overhead, almost catching her unaware. *Shut up and focus, Ruby, or you won't be alive to fulfill whatever that plan is.* She drew her sword and sent a thought to it, the idea of attacking the joins where the boulders connected. The personalities inside responded enthusiastically in her thoughts. She dashed in and slashed at the arm that came down to knock her flying, severing one of the small boulders that formed something analogous to a hand. The blow had struck directly at the join, and the sword disconnected the two. *Whatever magic animates that thing, my sword is sufficient to block it.* The stone fell to the floor, and she blasted it across the room and locked it away with the other one.

Idryll crowed, "Good one. Let me try." While the creature took another swing at Ruby, the tiger-woman sped in and slashed the back of his foot, one of her favorite locations. The single boulder that rested at the end of his leg disconnected as her claws passed through the space, and Ruby knocked it toward the others.

Now that they'd figured out the solution, the fight proved reasonable, except for the part where the boulder creature didn't seem to be injured or lose any energy or strength from their actions. Down to the moment they separated the last portion of his remaining limb from the torso, he spun, whirled, and smashed at them. He'd caught Ruby twice and sent her flying against the wall. Only the quick application of force magic to blunt the impact saved her from likely death. Her barrier faltered in one of those moments, and a few boulders tried to roll away, but Idryll put herself physically in their path, blocking them until Ruby could get them back under control.

When the final limb dropped, their foe stopped moving, and his remaining parts bowed. "Well done, *junra*, companion. I wish you luck in what lies beyond." The boulders disconnected and dropped, lifeless and inanimate again.

From above, Keshalla clapped. "Good show, you two." She leapt down over the balcony and landed with them. "As soon as he fell apart, some barrier vanished. Guess I was right about getting to be a spectator."

Ruby knelt and picked up a piece of stone that hadn't joined the rest, putting it in her pocket as a remembrance. Rising, she replied, "Who knows, maybe you'll get in the game later. For now, onward."

CHAPTER ELEVEN

The next chamber was sunken and about the same dimensions as the one previous, but with the floor a good ten feet below. A railing stopped them from walking off the entry ledge, and a series of pillars with flat tops at varying heights and distances from their location crossed the room. On the nearest column stood an owl, snowy white with accents of gray and eyes that displayed more intelligence than she'd ever seen in such a creature. Keshalla vanished and reappeared on the far side, on a matching ledge with a matching railing. She called, "Getting a little tired of being thrown around over here."

The owl ignored her comment and blinked its big eyes first at Ruby, then at Idryll. Its voice was higher than she'd guessed it would be, and it spoke with a strange accent she couldn't identify. "Welcome, *junra*. Welcome, companion. Congratulations on successfully overcoming the previous guardian."

Idryll asked, "Were you the partner of one of the *Mirra*?"

The old head inclined slightly toward her. "Indeed. *Mirra* Cashri and I spent many years together."

Ruby said, "Are you real? Or a spirit? A memory?"

"All of that and none of it. What I am is not relevant. The only thing that matters is the task ahead of you."

Idryll replied, "So, agility is part of the qualifications? If so, I'd be a much better choice than her."

The owl fluttered its wings, seeming amused. "You must cross the space safely to your friend."

Ruby asked, "Nothing more than that?"

The guardian confirmed, "Nothing more." It took off, soaring above in a lazy circle around the perimeter of the room.

She turned to Idryll and said, "Obviously, that can't be it. There has to be a trick, or test, or something else going on."

Her partner nodded. "Of course."

"I'll do a little experimenting. You stay here while I do."

"Perhaps I should be the one to try it."

Ruby shook her head. "Last time I checked, for all your agility, you can't protect yourself with a magic shield. I have multiple options in that category. If I fall, I won't get hurt." She wore the pendant under her outfit, ready to be called upon at need. Now she summoned the force shield that wrapped around her body an inch from her skin. *Okay, here we go.*

She estimated the jump from where she was to the nearest column as a foot or two longer than she was comfortable with, especially since the landing pad was only a couple of feet wide. She focused her magic and waved, creating a platform on the other side of the railing that extended from where they were to the first pedestal. The idea of using it to cross the whole room occurred to her, but she was confident they wouldn't outwit the test so easily. She pulled out her sword and poked at the magical surface to be sure it wasn't an illusion of what she intended, and it resisted appropriately. *Or appears to, anyway.*

Sheathing the weapon, she climbed up onto the railing and drew a deep breath. "Here goes nothing." She looked down before taking that first step, and something about the floor seemed strange. She reached into the pocket where she'd stashed her souvenir from the previous battle, pulled it out, and dropped it. It plummeted to and through the floor's surface, making noise once it was out of sight as if it bounced from object to object. She turned and met Idryll's eyes. "So, fake floor."

The shapeshifter nodded. "Yeah. Probably full of something nasty underneath. Like snakes."

She scowled. "It didn't sound like snakes. Sounded like metal. Spikes, maybe."

Her companion grinned. "Spike snakes. They stab you. Then they bite you."

Ruby rolled her eyes. "Quiet, you." She turned back toward the room. Motion in the corner of her eye caught her attention, and a moment later the owl plummeted through the air a few feet in front of her. Suddenly the platform she stood on vanished as if it'd never been. She was close enough to the pedestal that she was able to grab it with one hand and keep herself from falling, but barely. She pulled herself up and climbed into a wobbly crouch. "Not cool, featherhead." The guardian angled past again, and she swore that he wore a smile. She straightened when she thought her legs could safely hold her. "So, it's both a physical and a mental challenge."

Idryll replied, "If we have to rely on your brain, we're toast. Might as well go home."

Ruby countered, "Shut it and move ahead." The shapeshifter climbed the railing, but the moment she looked like she was about to leap, the owl darted in front of her to cut her off. The shapeshifter swiped at it with a hand, but it evaded easily.

Ruby muttered, "Oh, that's how it's going to be, is it?" She summoned a force platform and took a step onto it, then jumped lightly back as the guardian intervened. Idryll took the moment of distraction she'd created to leap to the next pillar, which was exactly what Ruby had expected. *Maybe it's about working together. Who knows? Unless something changes, I think we have it figured out.*

She summoned another platform and ran across, then leapt for the column as the owl arrived. In that fashion, they crossed the room, each of them making progress while the interfering avian was busy with the other. As they neared the far side, the distances became longer. Ruby threaded magic into her body, giving her a little extra speed and power, and noted that it didn't vanish when the owl flew by, even though her shield and platform did. *So, it can only mess with external magics. Good to know.*

When they finally reached the opposite side, Keshalla nodded in approval. "Well done. I was a little concerned you wouldn't see its strategy, but you picked up pretty quickly."

Ruby scowled. "I figured it out immediately. I don't know what you're talking about."

Idryll grinned. "You keep telling yourself that, Ruby."

The owl landed on the railing and spread its wings wide, flicking them ostentatiously before folding them back against his body. "Well done, *junra*. You overcame the two easiest challenges. Good luck in the room beyond."

She nodded. "Appreciated. So, what happens to you, now?"

The guardian cocked his head to the side. "For me, no time will pass between your exit from this room and the next *junra's* entrance, however long that may be on the outside."

Idryll replied, "Is this the destiny of all companions?" She sounded a little concerned.

The owl swiveled its gaze to the shapeshifter. "I do not know. I can only speak for myself, and the only other knowledge I have is that there is a room before mine and a room after, each with its challenges."

Keshalla asked, "Would you change your situation if you could?"

He flapped his wings at them. "I have no idea. Existing is far preferable to not existing. Without Cashri, one way to pass the time seems equivalent to any other."

Ruby felt a surge of empathy at the sense of loss that must've driven those words. "Be well, guardian."

"Thank you, *junra*."

She turned and headed through the doorway that led out of the space. The next room was a repeat of the first chamber. It dawned on her that they were in some sort of magical space, as there was no way the castle on the mountaintop could stretch this far in one direction. Awaiting them was a humanoid figure who looked vaguely like a Mist Elf but with some other bloodline in there. Idryll gave a soft growl at the sight of him, and he nodded at them. "Companion, *junra*, welcome to the third challenge. It will, sadly, be your last."

Ruby replied, "You mean this is the final challenge?"

He shook his head. "No. I mean you will fail it."

Idryll scowled. "He's a shapeshifter. I can smell it."

"Like you."

Her partner tilted her head to the side. "Have you also lost your natural form?"

Ruby blinked and turned to her. "What? What the hell are you talking about?"

Idryll gave a choked laugh. "I guess we never discussed it. Once upon a time, I was an elf. Then, for a long time, I was a tiger. Now I am truly neither, and yet both."

The other figure nodded. "Exactly my tale, but not a tiger, of course."

Keshalla asked, "What are you, then?"

He shrugged. "You'll know when the time is right. Or, you could simply leave now and avoid the pain and the screaming and such."

Ruby didn't like his attitude. "So, what's your deal? What do we have to do?"

"Get past me."

She laughed. "That doesn't seem that hard, three on one."

He smiled. "I wasn't speaking to you, *junra*." The world wrenched to the side, and suddenly Ruby found herself at the far end of the room, standing beside Keshalla, unable to move out of the small rectangular area defined by the carvings at their feet. She shouted, "Not fair."

He looked back over his shoulder. "The *junra and* the companion are a team. If one isn't worthy, neither is the other. You've proven you can work together, or you wouldn't have reached this place. Now it's time for her test."

Idryll laughed. "It's like Christmas, my birthday, and Halloween all wrapped into one. Bring it on, scumbag."

Ruby shouted, "Kick his ass," and the fight began.

CHAPTER TWELVE

Idryll shifted to become a tiger, somehow positive they would fight the battle on four legs. Her opponent shrank in height but spread out in stature, transforming into a black-furred wolf. His uniform ebon color was a stark contrast to her multi-hued coat. When he spoke, she finally got to see what everyone meant when they told her how strange it looked when she talked in her tiger form. A mouth not made for words accused, "You are unworthy."

With a hiss, she circled to her left. He mirrored the move, maintaining the distance between them. She countered, "If *you* were worthy, I'm doubly or triply so. Believe me. I haven't come this far and gone through this much only to fail my partner by losing to you, dog-face."

He laughed, and it sounded like a half-bark. "Many before you said the same, although more civilly. They, too, were incorrect." Unlike most of the opponents she faced while in this form, he was bigger than she was and as impressively muscled. It would require cleverness and instinct to defeat him. She feinted, but instead of backpedaling as she'd assumed he would, he responded aggressively. Claws scraped along the floor as he charged forward and snapped at her leg when she dodged sideways. *Faster than I expected.* She turned the dodge into a counterattack, swiping out a clawed paw at his side. He displayed a strange agility that spoke to his part-humanoid nature and leapt in a spinning flip to the side, rather than forward or back.

Apparently noting something in her expression, he gave another barking laugh. "When you've spent as long as I have in your various forms, they tend to run together."

"So you're saying you have the brain of an ordinary wolf and the reaction speed and instincts of an elf? That should make you fairly easy to defeat." Idryll rushed in during the beat in which he absorbed her message. She snapped at his front leg, catching it with a grazing blow that set him slightly off balance. She twisted and turned, her rear feet scrabbling in an arc as she drove herself toward him again.

Stars blossomed in her vision as he brought his head around to slam into hers from the side, a move she'd never seen an opponent on four legs use. She stumbled and went down, and he jumped on her back, his teeth scraping the back of her neck. She channeled magic instinctively to her muscles and threw herself sideways, landing on top of him before he rolled them over again. Her body didn't have enough strength to dislodge him, and those jaws were pushing his teeth in toward her spine.

Instead of futilely continuing to try to pitch him off, she transformed into her humanoid figure. His weight crushed down on her, but his jaws no longer trapped her smaller neck. She used the opening to stab her fingers back over her shoulder, claws extended and aimed at his eyes. He had no option but to jump aside, and by the time he had recovered to come back at her, she was fully a tiger again.

He offered her a nod. "Valid technique. Not bad."

She gave a derisive snort. "I'm only getting started, cupcake. Sure you don't want to give this up?"

He paused and cocked his head to the side for a moment. "You do understand what we're doing here, right? I could *never* give up, for if I did, an unworthy candidate might complete the full *venamisha*. Someone like that could do irreparable damage."

Idryll gave a sober bow, touching her nose to her paw. "I apologize. They were only combat words. I respect the sacrifice that keeps you present here."

"Then make it worth the effort, companion." He braced himself, and she charged. This time it was brute force against brute force as they met chest to chest, rearing up on back legs with muscles straining, biting and clawing at their opponent. A hard slice burned across her chest, blood flowing out immediately to stain her fur crimson. She returned a snap to his face that cut him above his eye, blood loss rendering him unable to see from that side. She landed on all four paws again and circled, but he moved faster than before, ensuring she couldn't get into his blind spot. He growled and thrashed as she darted in, snapping his teeth onto the paw that had been heading for his other eye. He wrenched it hard, and the joint snapped. She limped away, cursing herself for being overly impetuous.

They continued to circle, Idryll hopping to keep him from coming at her wounded side, him turning to protect his blind spot. She snarled, "I don't suppose we could call this over."

He swung his head from side to side. "It only ends in a defeat. Surrender from my side is unacceptable. You, of course, may give up whenever you like."

She pretended to stumble, and he flinched in toward her before he corrected. His response was almost fast enough to keep him safe, but not quite. She raked a claw down his side, opening his skin and giving his lifeblood another path to escape. He snarled, all pretense of civilization gone, and charged in at her, his teeth seeking her throat. Two options presented themselves, and she chose the one she figured would be less expected.

Idryll transformed into her human form and fell backward, her broken arm cradled against her body as she got her legs under his bulk. Her tiger muscles had stayed during the shape change, so she was able to hold his jaws away while her momentum carried her backward. She kicked out as her back rolled on the floor, pushing her legs out as powerfully as she could, and the wolf flew up and over her, then across the room to slam hard into the floor. She rose to her feet to continue the battle, but he was unconscious.

A moment later, a wave of magic swept over her, and her wound healed painlessly. When her vision cleared, he stood before her in his humanoid form and sketched a shallow bow. "Well done, companion. You overcame instinct and used wisdom. It is rewarding to see someone like me pass the test."

Idryll nodded. "Thank you, guardian. Good luck with

your future battles. You serve your partner well, even beyond his death."

He smiled and vanished, and Idryll walked over to the other two women. Keshalla said, "Nice move."

Ruby lifted an eyebrow. "You got that from *Star Trek*, didn't you? Watching old reruns of William Shatner throwing around poorly costumed aliens."

Her partner laughed. "I'll never tell." She gestured with her chin at the doorway that lay beyond. "I wonder, what do you think we'll find through there?"

Ruby shrugged. "I don't know, but I'm sure whatever it is, we're up to the task."

The three turned and headed forward into the next room. It proved to be even grander than the ones they'd been in, a massive library with three stories of books wrapping around in a circle. Wooden stairs climbed from level to level. Where the rest of the castle had been dark, cold stone, this space was warm and inviting. Idryll groaned. "They're going to ask you to read. How did they know your secret weakness?"

Ruby replied, "Har har, very funny. In any case, it doesn't look too scary in here. Maybe we're past the hardest part of the test."

A pair of large wingback chairs near the room's far end had their backs facing the entrance. A fox suddenly leapt onto the top of one, then sat and stared at them. "Oh, I wouldn't say that, *junra*. Of all the rooms you've faced, rest assured, this will be the most dangerous."

CHAPTER THIRTEEN

Ruby gave a soft sigh and tried not to let her irritation at the process of the *venamisha* show through. "Wow, what a shock. I'm Ruby, this is Idryll, and the one browsing the books over there is Keshalla." Her mentor had stepped away immediately to examine the shelves.

Her partner whispered, "Never saw her as much of a reader. More likely to hit someone with a book than open it."

She nodded. "Me neither, but she is crazy smart, so not a huge shock."

The fox responded, "The good news is that you have reached your final challenge. Succeed in this test, and you will have completed the trials."

A surge of anticipation washed through her. "Really? All of them?"

The creature replied crossly, "Indeed. I believe that's what I said."

Ruby straightened and strode forward, feeling Idryll doing the same slightly behind and to her right. She stopped at a respectful distance. "So, what is the situation here?"

He smiled. "Nothing complicated. You must defeat me to complete your test."

She frowned. "No offense, but you don't seem like a particularly strong fighter in that form." After the shapeshifter in the previous room, she was well aware he probably wasn't revealing all of his abilities.

He tilted his head slightly to the side. "No, with that, I cannot argue. Are you prepared?"

Ruby looked over at Idryll, who nodded. She turned back to the fox. "I am."

"Very good. The battle will be fought on a different plane, but know that should you die there, your body here dies, as well. In that likely event, the observer shall be portaled back with her memories of the castle and what has transpired in it removed."

Keshalla looked back over her shoulder and scowled. "Messing with other people's minds is not cool."

The fox flicked his tail but didn't reply to the other woman. Instead, he addressed his final comments directly to her and Idryll. "Good luck, Ruby Achera, companion."

The transition from the library to a different place happened without fanfare. One second, Ruby stood in the comfortable room surrounded by books. The next, she stood in a broken landscape surrounded by mass quantities of nothingness. Red earth and black rocks abounded, the former dusty and dry, the latter sharp enough to cut. She muttered, "Obsidian, maybe, or something similar. I don't like the looks of those edges."

Idryll replied, "Agreed." The ground trembled, and a small hole five feet in front of them discharged a jet of steam that shot ten feet in the air and sustained for several seconds before falling away. Even from their distance, the heat of the eruption was palpable. Her partner continued, "Looks as if lethal steam is on the menu, as well. I'm not going to lie. I *really* don't like this place. Let's go back and fight the wolf guy again."

Ruby chuckled. "Probably not an option. Although I'm not sure who we're fighting." The answer came from a short distance away as the fox, now double the size of any of its species she'd ever seen, emerged from behind one of the rock projections. She muttered, "Too easy. There's gotta be a trick here." It revealed itself a moment later as a cacophony of voices repeated the first fox's phrase, and a dozen more of the creatures appeared from hiding spots all around them. She drew her sword and dagger and turned in a slow circle to gauge the enemy's numbers and positions. "So, that's a lot." In the corner of her eye, she saw Idryll's claws emerge, and her muscles grow and lengthen as she readied herself for battle. Ruby called, "Any rules?"

One of the foxes off to the left replied, "Only that you die, *junra*." Its voice was harsher, nastier sounding than the other guardians' had been. *I wonder if these are all different beings, or if they're separate elements of a single being's personality or some other thing entirely. Maybe I can find out afterward. If there is a later.*

The foxes moved, and Ruby and Idryll flowed in a practiced motion to stand back-to-back. She summoned a force shield around them both, leaving a tiny gap through which she could cast spells. She thrust the dagger through it and sent a wash of fire at the nearest pair of foxes, catching them in mid-charge. One was tan. The other had a coat that vaguely resembled the orange in her partner's fur. *Funny what you notice at times like this.*

The creatures ran through her magic as if it wasn't even there, entirely unsinged. It didn't take her mind long to jump from that realization to the conclusion that her shield wouldn't be particularly valuable against them, either. She shouted, "Scatter," and ran to the right. *Well, this just got a lot more difficult.*

Idryll ran forward at Ruby's command. She angled toward a trio of foxes that had clustered together, prepared to slash them to ribbons. Her instincts warned her of impending danger, and she threw herself instantly to the right in a spinning jump. Had she continued on her original course, the explosion of fire and steam that blasted out of the ground would've fully engulfed her. As it was, she took a painful burn along her left arm, which drew a surprised yelp. *Well, that's embarrassing.* She landed cleanly and flipped into a cartwheel in case anyone had been aiming for her landing spot.

When she stopped moving, two of the foxes were in close range, and the third was vanishing toward her back in her peripheral vision. She picked one and moved at him, angling to put him in the way of his partner so they couldn't both attack at once. He jumped with his teeth bared, going straight for her throat. She smashed an arm across his trajectory, blocking his effort and knocking him aside while positioning herself for the strike from his partner that had to be coming.

The other fox went for her leg, and she leapt forward over it, sensing the pack hunting instinct at work. *The front two distract me while the third one rips out my Achilles tendon. It's the strategy I'd use.* She angled the jump so she would land near the one she'd batted aside, who was scrambling to regain his feet. She channeled the momentum of the move into a kick that sent him flying. There was no question that something inside him had broken, and he was out of the fight. On the one hand, she felt bad about it. The foxes were smaller and less well-armed, and *dammit to hell*, cute. On the other, they were trying to kill her, so there was only so much goodwill their novelty could buy.

She spun and found the other two stalking toward her again, having been joined by a second pair. "Four on one? A couple more friends and maybe it will be a fair fight." They uttered a sound much like laughing and suddenly increased in size, a ripple through their body that left them bigger when it had passed. She sighed and muttered, "Sure, just had to open your mouth, didn't you, Idryll?"

Ruby was surprised at the creatures' agility. She'd figured they would be nimble, but the way they were able to twist and turn and redirect their flight while in midair was entirely unexpected. One gave her a nasty bite on her cheek when she'd thought it would pass harmlessly by while she defended against another and somehow caught her, anyway. She swung her sword in a wide, low arc, spinning in a circle to clear the surrounding area. The one who jumped at her face during that maneuver got a dagger strike in the side for its trouble and fell away, bleeding. *Don't feel guilty, Ruby. They're not really animals, and even if they were, they're trying to kill you.* She received a warning from her sword's inhabitants and lashed out blindly to her right, cleanly cutting a fox in half as it went for her neck. Suddenly her opponents doubled in size, ratcheting up the danger to a substantially greater level. She called, "Watch out, they get bigger."

Idryll's reply was a short laugh, followed by, "Thanks for the information. Already aware."

"You could've shared."

"Little busy over here, no time to talk."

Ruby had been turning a slow circle, keeping her sword pointed at anyone who looked like they might charge. She'd apparently done so for long enough that her movements had become predictable. A heavy weight hit her in the back, and she felt teeth at the nape of her neck. She dove forward in a roll, losing the dagger as her wrist slammed off a small, thankfully non-bladed rock in her path and numbed her hand. She came up angry and summoned her magic, willing it into her muscles and bloodstream to increase her speed. Her blade flashed out as she went on the offensive, and her enemies responded by splitting away and coming back at her from several directions at once. She called, "Rotate," and dashed toward Idryll.

At the command, Idryll turned and ran toward Ruby's position. One tactic they practiced seemingly endlessly was switching opponents during a battle, and Idryll ran at the trio of foxes that remained of her partner's foes. The nearest tried to scramble away, clearly caught off guard. However, she was faster than Ruby, faster than the fox could have expected, and she slammed a brutal kick into his side that sent him into another. She shouted, "Goal," and spun to smash a backfist into the body that was flying at her back. He hit the ground hard and didn't rise. "Similar instincts, buddy, unfortunately for you."

The lone remaining fox doubled in size, and Idryll shook her head. "Seems unfair that when you knock out a small one, you get a bigger one." She drove in, attacking with teeth and claws. It met her furious rush, scoring blows as it took her to the ground and used its back legs to rake at her. She snarled and transformed into her full tiger form, matching the attack. They each rolled aside to disengage, and both came up bleeding. Idryll growled, "Surrender."

The fox smiled, and it looked like the face of the guardian from the library. "Not an option. Defeat me or die. Oh, and did I mention this is a test for you both? If one of you dies, so does the other."

Sarcasm filled her mind. *Well, I had considered giving up and dying, but if it also means my partner fails, I guess I'll keep fighting. Idiot fox. Worst combat taunt ever.* Idryll set her feet, gathered her strength, and charged.

CHAPTER FOURTEEN

Ruby was pleased to see that Idryll had reduced her opponents to four but would have loved seeing a smaller number. *One, maybe. I'm sure I can handle one of the little guys with no problem.* She positioned her sword in front of her defensively and maneuvered to keep all four of them in sight, backpedaling when they tried to circle her. *That's a good way to get burned, Ruby. Literally.*

She stopped and reached out with her force magic, grabbing her dagger and pulling it toward her, then adding more force behind it to magically hurl the weapon at the fox closest to it. The blade pinioned it in the hip, and that foe went down, out of the fight. The other three snarled and charged her as one. She got the sword in the way of the first, its claws scraping off the metal and a yelp of pain signaling that the blade had scored. She ducked under the second one as it leapt high toward her throat. Its paws tangled in her hair as it arrested its motion and jerked her backward.

The punch she had aimed at the third only scraped it,

thanks to the involuntary stumble. She shouted "Kagji" reflexively, then cursed when she remembered that magic didn't faze the foxes. She lifted her arm and whipped the sword around her head, blade pointing straight down, and felt the creature jump away. A hunk of her hair fluttered through the air as she spun to find him and finish the job, but he was already out of range. *Should've brought my dart bracelet. Or pistol. Or maybe some grenades. Sure do wish we had some grenades.* Even with her magically increased speed, the creatures were faster than she could ever be.

Ruby spotted a hole nearby and ran for it, hoping that proximity triggered the steam jets. She screamed as if in fear, trying to entice her enemies to follow, then dove at an angle away from it as the pillar of super-heated vapor materialized. A screech from behind told her that at least one fox hadn't managed to dodge. When she turned back, the one with her dagger in its hip and the two that were still active had all grown larger by a third. "Not fair," she growled.

Idryll had already figured they would both have to live to win the challenge. She knew that *Mirra* Kaeni's companion had been a fox, and the notion that the guardians they'd faced were all previous companions had seemed like a logical conclusion. Thus, companions had to be worthy as well. She and her foe were now evenly matched in size, and both were similarly injured. The burn she'd taken had healed some during her shape change and was now nothing more than a minor annoyance and distraction.

She circled, snapping at his tail when he didn't move quite fast enough and yanking before he twisted and pulled it away. He turned to her with an expression that seemed to say, "Really?" and barreled in at her. Part of her wanted to meet that charge head-on, but she leapt instead, waiting until he was committed to the motion to take to the air. Her claws slashed at his back as she flew over him, and she landed in a twisting skid on the dry earth. He was already inbound again, the new furrows in his flesh not seeming to bother him in the least. He whipped out an arm and clawed at her, the attack unexpected since she'd focused on his teeth. *Stupid.* She took cuts on her flank, but they were shallow and not immediately worrisome. *By the time I bleed out, this fight will be over. We'll either have won or lost a different way.*

Idryll was starting to get the impression that she was only strong enough to keep the creature at bay and decided that should be her strategy until Ruby told her differently. She shifted tactics, staying crouched, feinting and fading, avoiding his attacks instead of meeting them. His style changed in response. The oversized fox's efforts became faster and less powerful, clearly hoping to catch her in an evasion. It was the right call since one good lick could potentially slow her sufficiently for him to finish the fight. However, Idryll had been in battles like this before, and there was no way a fox, no matter how big he was, was going to beat a tiger in a war that resembled a hunt.

Ruby spotted Idryll facing off against a giant fox. She knew that if she didn't act quickly and didn't take out the pair in front of her simultaneously, their remaining enemies' growth would put them at a severe disadvantage. She sped into a run again, this time toward her partner, around one of the obsidian-like rock formations. Stopping on the far side of it, she sheathed her sword and pumped energy into her muscles. She gave a loud shout and kicked at the rock, hoping it shared a certain fragility with its Earthly cousin when attacked from the right angle. Her target splintered and flew, shards jetting out at the pair of foxes following her. They fell, bleeding profusely, pierced in a half dozen places each. She spun at a roar from the other direction and saw that the fox facing Idryll had doubled in size again, now taller than she was despite its four-legged stance. Ruby charged, and Idryll did the same, circling to the opposite side before making her rush to force their foe to choose between them.

The fox selected her and nimbly blocked the sword strike she sent at it, her blade lopping off one of its claws while the rest of them stopped her blow before it could do any real damage. The creature lurched forward, snapped its body around at the last minute to slam into her, and sent her flying. She landed between the smaller foxes and among the shrapnel that had killed them. The sharp stones slashed into both her hands and the back of her head.

She ignored the wounds and got back to her feet, pumping more magic into her body and using her free hand to scrabble at the potions on her left thigh as she moved in an unsteady run back toward the fight. The over-sized creature had thwarted Idryll's attack from behind, and she was circling it, dashing in to nip at its legs but skittering back out of range to avoid its blocks. Ruby didn't think she'd have adequate strength to administer a killing blow in one strike, and without her magic to finish the job, she wasn't sure she'd survive long enough to end her opponent. *So, I need a different option. Unfortunately, there's only one left that might work.*

She gritted her teeth and opened her mind to the sword, imploring the beings within to help her. Then she released the Atlantean representation of the artifact into her mind as she called upon its power. He crowed with glee, and she felt battle lust surge as the shadow tendrils reached out to wrap around the fox. He turned in surprise at the presence of functioning magic. *These things don't follow the same rules as other magic, which is mostly bad but useful at this moment.* She tightened the tendrils and stalked toward him, ready to slice his throat and end the fight. When she got near enough to administer that final stroke, he vanished, and suddenly they were in the library again. Ruby's legs wobbled, and she fell, only then realizing that the wounds to her hands and head were far worse than they'd seemed and had come back from that other place with her. *Channeling too much magic to my body to notice. Keshalla warned me. Stupid.*

Through blurry eyes, she saw the fox, still in position on top of the chair, gazing down at her. Her focus was only for him, but she did note a hand opening the pouch containing her potions and knew her allies would keep her from death if anyone could. She had no energy remaining to do anything and felt like she'd burned away a core part of herself.

He announced, "Your trials are over. You have proven yourselves adequate to follow in the steps of those who have gone before. A messenger will arrive to lead you the rest of the way." He gave a respectful nod to her and Idryll, holding each for several seconds. "You are now able to portal out of this place."

Liquid trickled into her mouth, and she felt the healing potion begin its work on her damaged body. *Messenger, is it? That could be a day, a year, a decade away. Not going to hold my breath.*

Idryll's voice came as if through a long tunnel. "Let's portal her back to the village so she can rest."

Ruby murmured, "That sounds like a great idea," and heard her words as a bunch of slurred, mostly unintelligible syllables. She concentrated and managed to force a few coherent sentences out before she lost consciousness. "Grab a book or three. Anything that looks interesting. The archivist will be ticked if she finds out we were in a library and didn't bring her books."

CHAPTER FIFTEEN

Julianna Sloane rose from the couch in her Las Vegas apartment with a smile as her lieutenants entered. She hugged each of them, part of the "New me, new rules" attitude she was trying to take with her people. It would be some time before she felt like dating or being social with anyone other than those who worked for her, so she wanted to ensure that those relationships were as strong as they could be. She gestured the pair to the couch, another change from previous practices, and served them both coffee from the pot she'd had sent up. When they were all arranged, she said, "So. Bring me up to date."

Smith began the report. "Things here are secure. We're getting along well with the people who own the building. They've granted us access to all the security feeds, and one of our staff is now watching them at all times. Plus, we're running surveillance programs we brought with us from Reno."

Julianna nodded. Her husband had been justifiably paranoid and hadn't scrimped on the security in their casino penthouse. Their surveillance and defensive tech were top-notch. He continued, "I think it's safe to say we now have a reliably secure base of operations here. Our people are checking into the restaurants you asked about, making sure we know who's working in the back, and discussing arrangements for possible visits." Another of her husband's fears had been poison, a tactic he'd used on multiple occasions in his previous career. So, before she would eat at a restaurant, she would need to be certain no assassins lay in wait for her to give them an opportunity. For now, she'd brought her chef from Reno along, and trusted employees were buying supplies in other cities and bringing them back to Vegas.

"Excellent. And our operations in Ely?"

Thompson nodded and took over the speaking role. "Aces did a nice job of knocking the security company the Council invited in back on its heels. The partners report that they made off with a great deal of new tech and injured quite a few of their operatives."

"Only injured?"

Thompson shrugged. "That's what they said. Of course, they also blew up the building, so anyone who didn't escape beforehand is probably rather more than injured."

Julianna laughed. "Well, well. I didn't think they had that level of nastiness in them. I bet it was the dwarf's idea." The others nodded. "He seems the more bloodthirsty of the two. Although," she thought of herself and her husband, "looks can be deceiving. Anyway, good. What did we learn about the other company?"

Smith shrugged. "From what the Aces people said, the Worldspan folks fought well. We've been checking into them, and they seem quite competent. They come with outstanding recommendations from a large number of clients."

"Anyone we know?"

He shook his head. "Mainly Utah. The boss, uh, the previous boss, hadn't put much effort in there yet."

She laughed softly. "Well, maybe that will be the next market we move into once we finish up north. So, do you think it's worth seeing if we can get this other company on our side?"

Her lieutenants looked at each other. Smith shrugged, and Thompson nodded. The latter said, "From what we've heard, they probably won't respond at all well to having been attacked. Chances are strong they'll increase their efforts in Ely, rather than stepping them down."

Julianna nodded. "Good. I think this has potential. You should drop in on them."

Thompson lifted an eyebrow. "Unannounced?"

"Sure. Let's see how they respond to the unexpected."

Thompson was in the passenger seat as Smith drove. They'd rented a helicopter for the quick trip from city to city, then rented a car at the airport. A large black SUV was their chosen conveyance, in case they needed its power or its toughness if things went awry. She certainly didn't expect a social visit to turn into anything bad and doubted the vehicle selection would matter much if it did. Still, it didn't take long in the security business to learn that you always prepared as if it would. *Especially when working for someone like the Sloanes.*

She'd spent time in the military and kicked around in a couple of mercenary units masquerading as government-contracted security companies before taking the gig for the Sloane family. The employees who worked under her and Smith were an almost equal mix between people who had come up through criminal organizations and those who had been military or law enforcement and decided to make a change. She'd experienced enough of the seedy side of life to not feel too many moral compunctions about what the Sloanes were into. On the rare occasions when she drank enough to get brutally honest, she would accuse *everyone* of being a criminal and explain that when everyone was, no one was. Those episodes usually ended with fists flying and furniture breaking.

Smith said, "One minute out," as if she wasn't already tracking their progress on her phone as she paged through the Worldspan Security records their infomancer had provided. *That's one really good thing we got out of working with the Aces people, the connection to Scimitar. She's the sharpest computer jockey I've ever worked with.* The car stopped at a gated security booth, and Smith said, "Representatives of Julianna Sloane, here to meet with someone from Worldspan."

The guard, clad in a bulletproof vest and with a rifle hanging across his chest, nodded. "Hang on, let me check." They'd debated having Scimitar create a fictitious back-dated appointment for them, making them seem legit until they got inside, but had decided the people they wanted to talk to were more likely to be annoyed than impressed with such a tactic. So they'd chosen the more respectful route. After several moments, the guard hit the button to open the heavy metal gates and waved them forward. "Pull in over there."

"Over there," was a concrete pad off to the side of the two-lane road that ran into the industrial park. Smith complied, and when the vehicle was solidly in place on the slab, a barrier of spikes that would shred their tires if they tried to drive over them shot up around the border of it to keep them immobile. Thompson nodded. "Clever. Not a bad plan if you have the space for it and don't care about ticking off your visitors."

Another SUV much like theirs pulled up, and two men climbed out, both with hands resting on pistols in drop holders. Thompson and Smith opened their doors slowly and climbed out of the vehicle, keeping their arms spread away from their bodies. A third person appeared from the SUV and patted them down, noting the guns in their shoulder holsters but not taking them. He informed them mildly, "You'll have to leave those in the lobby. We'll give you a receipt." He seemed like law enforcement, in his forties, probably with military in his background. The other two, both younger, felt the same to her.

She gave him a quick nod. "Whatever it takes. Smith, don't forget the case."

Her partner opened the back door and pulled out a briefcase. The man asked, "What's in it?"

Smith replied, "The usual. Some papers for a proposal, a laptop, nothing exciting."

The other nodded. "It stays with you until we get to the lobby, where we will thoroughly inspect it. Any questions?"

Thompson shook her head. "We're in your hands."

They rode in the back seat, with one of the men next to them and the other two up front. Their seatmate was twisted to face them and had liberated his gun from its holster, holding it calmly against his leg. *Professional. They do things right. That's a good sign.* When they reached the lobby, they entered what was essentially an airlock, with heavy glasslike doors on either side. She guessed it was bulletproof glass, if not something tougher. Smith put the briefcase into a scanner as directed, and the guards stood and waited after casually taking positions that would allow them to shoot without creating a crossfire.

With no visible sign of communication, the one who seemed in charge said, "Okay, it's cleared, you can grab it. Go in, turn to your left, and surrender your guns." Once they did, their escort brought them beyond the single set of doors that led on from the lobby. The man who'd been their conversational partner led them, and the pair that had accompanied him trailed behind. He explained, "Boss isn't available yet, so she asked me to give you the dime tour." He took them through the building, a strange three-story combination of bunker chic and corporate modernism. The walls were painted and decorated as they would be in any business park, but when passing through doorways, Thompson noted they were twice as thick as they would have been in a more innocent place.

The doors were all open, but she imagined when they shut, they would have some serious locking mechanisms that snapped automatically into place. Small camera domes were present throughout the facility. *Probably why all these doors are open for us. Someone is charting our progress and making it happen.* Their escort took them through meeting rooms, a modest cafeteria, and into a garage on the first floor, which held five black SUVs and several vehicles of other sizes. They ranged from what looked like an armored car to a Winnebago-sized command center, to judge by the communication antennas on the top.

The second floor turned out to be offices, many of them filled with people sitting behind computers. It appeared to be a stereotypical tech business until you peered closer and realized that every worker was a little harder-looking than you'd expect. The third floor comprised a wide-open meeting space in the middle, with couches and a table, a large conference room along one wall, and two offices along the other. Their research had indicated that the company had two principals, and the man took them into the office of the one who, according to their information, had been present in Magic City prior to the attack on their headquarters there.

The elf rose from behind her desk and extended a hand, moving comfortably toward them, showing no signs of injury from the fight with Aces. Thin dark braids hung down over her shoulders, and her leather pants and tunic definitely weren't business casual. They exchanged introductions, and she moved back to her chair, gesturing for them to take the ones across the desk from her. She asked, "So, what can I do for the family of The Nightmare?"

Smith slowly lifted the briefcase and set it on the desk. He said, "Our boss has an offer for you. Is it okay if I open this?"

She casually drew a pistol from an open desk drawer and pointed it at him, then nodded. He opened the case, pressing the almost invisible button to release the concealed compartment. Inside, hidden from physical scans by advanced technology that had cost a serious amount to procure, was an encrypted video communication link strong enough to get past the jamming field surrounding the headquarters. On the large display was Julianna Sloane, who grinned out of the screen at the three of them. "Ms. Prash, thank you for agreeing to meet with us. I have a proposition that I think you're going to find very interesting."

CHAPTER SIXTEEN

Jared Trenton hit the button on the pod coffee maker to brew something strong and dark. The aftermath of their attack on Worldspan Security had involved a lot of pitching, a lot of calls, and a whole lot of effort. He'd been going on minimal sleep for several days, and even though he'd always thrived on overwork, he was starting to feel the effects. He inhaled the coffee's bitter fumes, sipped it, and sighed. "Okay, I can function now."

He took his chair at the small table in the secure room at the Aces Security headquarters. The featureless white walls were a balm to his nerves. His partner, Grentham, was already seated, looking far less tired than Jared felt. They'd both been on a high since taking on the bigger company.

The dwarf said, "Gotta love how Worldspan has pretty much gone silent since we dropped in and bashed them down. Not exactly a strong response."

Jared nodded. "But one that definitely works in our favor. You know, we lucked out on that op. Everything went right. The infomancer played a big role in that. We need to make sure she's happy."

"We could send her a bonus payment."

Jared shook his head. "Impersonal. Let's give her something from the pile of stuff we liberated. There's doubtless an item in there that would pique her interest."

Grentham laughed. "Liberated? Good word. I'd say we outright stole it."

Jared chuckled. "Either way, it belongs to us now."

Apparently overwhelmed with jealousy of Jared's drink, Grentham rose to make his own. "A lot of that stuff is going to be useful for the new gigs we'll be getting."

"Yeah, spreading the information about how they weren't able to protect their building swung the pendulum away from them. Our other competitors are making some deals too, but I think it'll fall out with us having the lion's share."

Grentham grunted. "The thing with the Mist is still right in the front of everybody's mind. Blowing up the place was a good choice."

Jared nodded. "Aside from the insurance company and Worldspan personnel, it was a clean op with no bystanders harmed. Like I said, a definite win." He drank his coffee in silence until his partner sat across the table from him again.

The dwarf replied, "You know, I promised my people a cut to help out. They take cash."

Jared sighed. "We're not doing great on financial reserves at the moment. We'll need to liquidate some of the items we've *liberated* then, maybe including the gems." He gestured toward the diamonds they had stolen from Spirits casino, which had more or less become their albatross. As long as they kept them in the secure room where no one could track them, the gems did no harm. If they risked taking them out, though, they opened themselves up to trouble. *A fortune in stones and no way to sell them. Well, eventually, things will quiet down enough that we can manage it. Perhaps we can bring someone in here to do the buy.*

His partner offered, "I can take care of turning the items into money. I have some small skills in the area."

Jared laughed. "If I didn't know you so well, I'd say you were using Aces as a way to fund your little trade empire."

The dwarf joined in the laughter. "I can see that. Like you said, either way. As long as everything goes right for both of us, it's all good. Speaking of which, we better get a move on if we're going to make it to Invention on time."

Jared rose and stretched. "I can't even imagine what a board meeting populated exclusively by gnomes would be like."

Grentham grinned. "Same as any other, I bet, but shorter. Don't be speciesist. Bodies differ, but in the end, people are all the same. Promise them the moon at a decent price point, and greed will win out."

"Well then, let's go make that happen."

They entered by the front door of the technology-themed gnome casino, which was kind of a cross of steampunk and nerd culture. Of all the casinos on the strip, it was Jared's least favorite. He thought it was noisier, more cluttered, less elegant, and far more outright annoying than any of the others. He muttered, "A couple of hours in here, and I'd lose my mind."

Grentham laughed. "I don't know. I kind of dig this place. If we do put people in here, they're going to need earplugs. I imagine it would be possible to set up an algorithm that filters out the normal sounds or at least dampens them. Maybe we can get some branded earpieces like rock stars wear."

They had only made it a dozen feet inside before a pair of gnomes in uniform intercepted them. They were both short, typical for their species, but other than that looked equal parts smart and menacing. Their hands rested on a pistol-shaped weapon of some sort on their belt, but he couldn't make out what filled the holster. *Taser, probably, but who knows? Could be magitech.* He had enough self-awareness to realize that question might be the real reason the place made him so uncomfortable. He had a firm grasp on technology, far more than the average person. He also had a good understanding of magic, at least how to use it and how to defend against it, and felt adept in that environment. Mixing the two...*that* was a recipe for chaos, in his estimation.

The slightly taller of the two gnomes nodded at them. "Mr. Jared. Mr. Grentham. Please, come with us."

Unlike the other casinos, which generally had grand sweeping staircases leading from the first to the second level, the gnomes had elevators that looked like old-school pneumatic tubes but festooned with brass and rivets and who knew what else. They stepped into a capsule, the door rotated closed in front of them, and they shot up several levels. The casino itself was four stories, the hotel rising much higher beyond it. Floors one and two were the public areas. The third floor was open to gnomes only, a decision that caused some consternation among the Council, his partner had said. The gnomes valued their privacy and didn't budge on the issue. He imagined games of chance using technological and magical items that would be outlawed if commonly employed.

Their destination was the fourth floor, which turned out to be a fairly standard office setup, though slightly smaller in scale than the ones he was used to. The design had taken into account that humans and even Kilomea might visit from time to time, but things generally trended toward serving the gnomes' stature. They were escorted to a conference room and left there, and Jared grimaced at his partner as he lowered himself into a seat that seemed too small to bear his weight.

Grentham said, "Interesting place. I'd really like to see what's on the third floor. Hell, it would be worth giving them a discount to find out."

Jared laughed. "Whatever it takes to seal the deal. Once we get our claws in them, then we can ratchet things up. Especially if the other options around town diminish as they have been lately." He was aware they were probably being listened to, but he wasn't worried about it. *All part of the plan.* He figured the gnomes already held a low estimation of him, so playing into that expectation would only serve him well in the long run. *Makes me look truthful.* Besides, the process he described was how everyone played the game. The casino owners did it themselves on the gaming floors below. They caught people with the blinking lights and loud noises of the slot machines set to pay out with only the tiniest profit, then drew them in for the more expensive games of chance once they felt lucky. That was where the casino made its *real* money. *Might not be how it works in other places, but Magic City plays by its own rules.*

He rose again as a female gnome entered. She had bright red curly hair, an attractive face, and a curvy form wrapped in an appropriately scaled business suit in red and black. She waved at them. "Please, gentlemen, sit. No need for formality here. It's my hope we can get our business done quickly and profitably for both sides."

Grentham reclaimed his seat. "Music to my ears, Ms. Melinda."

She inclined her head as she sat on the opposite side of them. "So, tell me what you offer that's different from what everyone else offers. Don't start with price. Everyone's all about how they can save us money. I'm concerned about not becoming the next Mist. If it takes knocking down the payout on a few games to accomplish it, I have no problem with that."

They'd agreed that Grentham should lead. His partner said, "Well, as the only magical-owned security company in town, we have a unique understanding of your needs. We take pride in becoming part of your place, melding into the background so as not to distract your gamers. At the same time, we bring both cutting-edge technology and powerful knowledge of magic to the table. You can rest assured that these set us far beyond the capabilities of the human-owned companies, even the ones that have magicals on their staff."

He spread his hands apart in an open, oft-practiced gesture. "We know every piece of the puzzle intuitively.

Our people are largely ex-military and ex-law enforcement and have undergone rigorous rounds of testing to ensure they don't have any anti-magical bias." That was true. It was one of the things Grentham had insisted upon early in their partnership, and it had paid substantial dividends over time.

The gnome nodded and turned her gaze to him. "Do you speak, Mr. Jared?"

He chuckled. "I do, but I find that my partner is much more adept at it. I endorse everything he said. I hope we can reach an agreement that is long-term and beneficial for us all."

She grinned. "Well, your initial pitch gives us a starting point. Let me call for some lunch, and we'll get down to the details."

CHAPTER SEVENTEEN

Ruby opened the door of her bedroom at her parents' house with a groan. Idryll wrapped an arm around her waist to steady her, and Ruby leaned on the other woman. Simply getting herself showered and dressed had been a challenge. She didn't feel like the last part of the *venamisha* had caused her permanent damage, but it was fair to say she hurt as much as she had after any fight or training session, even given the healing potion her allies had administered. She'd considered downing another, but Keshalla had cautioned her to let her body do what it needed to do. Ruby couldn't argue with the sentiment. Sometimes pushing with magic led to unintended consequences.

The octopus tattoo on her arm, in particular, ached like the bone underneath was broken. She was expending constant mental effort to push the illusory Atlantean back into his glass box, but he was resistant to being re-imprisoned. She would probably need to spend an hour meditating at the bunker to do more than achieving a stalemate.

For now, she was hungry and hurting, felt as if she was trapped inside her flesh, and missed her family.

Matthias intercepted them halfway down. "Miss Ruby. Are you okay?"

She smiled, as the sight of him always made her happy. "Overdid it a little in combat practice yesterday. Nothing big. This, by the way, is my companion, Idryll."

He nodded. "Hello, Miss Idryll."

The shapeshifter, currently in her Mist Elf form with that flowing orange and red hair that made Ruby look plain beside her, gave him a friendly grin. "Well met, Matthias. Ruby has told me a lot about you. It's clear you've hidden a lot of her misdeeds over the years." They'd decided not to reveal that Idryll was the cat who had shared her bedroom on occasion. That would create too much confusion. History didn't specify that the *Mirra's* companion had to be a magical animal of some kind, and she wasn't sure the boulder creature fit into that category, anyway. She was willing to use that lack of evidence to keep Idryll's true nature a mystery for now. He laughed and fell behind as they continued.

Her parents rose at the sight of her stiff entrance into the room, and she lifted a hand with a smile. "I'm fine, I'm fine, don't worry. Everyone, this is Idryll. Idryll, everyone." Morrigan raised an eyebrow and offered a small grin, and the others said hello. Her mother asked, "What's going on? We didn't expect you."

Ruby nodded and lowered herself into her chair. Idryll sat on the empty one to her left. "So, you know how I wasn't really able to talk about the *venamisha* before? Now I am." She related the tale as they ate breakfast, frequently pausing to stuff French toast into her mouth. "So, I think it's over. Three stages seem to be what everyone agrees upon, so I shouldn't have to do it again. Which is good because that last one hurt like a, uh, hurt a lot."

Her mother said, "Idryll came from those trials somehow?"

Ruby nodded. "Apparently, it's part of being worthy, being able to deal with smart-assed beings."

Idryll hurled the napkin at her face. "Well, if you would ever show the slightest bit of sense, maybe I wouldn't have to be the one doing all the heavy mental lifting."

The table erupted in laughter, and Dralen shook his head with a grin. "Seems like you have my sister down pat." Shifting his attention to her, he asked, "So, what, you're going to be the boss of everything?" He sounded a little annoyed.

Ruby shrugged. "Don't know. That wasn't made clear. I'll have responsibilities of some kind."

Morrigan wore a concerned expression, the corners of her mouth turning down slightly. "Will you have to spend more time on Oriceran? Or move there?" The concern in her voice probably read as fear of missing her to her parents, but Ruby knew her worry was more about the battle they waged for the safety of Magic City.

She shrugged. "There's supposed to be a messenger or something to let me know what's next. Based on prior experience, I have no guess at all as to how long that will take. I'm going to ignore the issue until the messenger arrives."

Her father, Rayar, asked, "Do you have any indication as to what those responsibilities might entail?"

She shook her head. "No idea. The mystics are looking into it, but it appears no one ever made a concerted effort to pass down that particular knowledge."

Her mother sighed, but it was a happy sound. "Once it's all official, we'll have to admit we've been less than truthful about you being a human. Plus, you won't have to wear a disguise anymore."

Ruby laughed. "Sometimes the disguise is useful. The rest of it is all you." She pointed at them. "Dishonest parents, lying to your friends and coworkers. Shameful." Laughter circled the table again.

Morrigan wasn't fully joining in the mirth, but she seemed to be trying. "Do you get a castle?"

She gave an imperious nod. "I'm sure of it. I decree castles for everyone when I'm in charge. You won't be able to walk down the street without bumping into another castle."

Dralen remarked, "So I guess you'll be stepping away from the family business, then?"

Ruby laughed. "Sorry to crush your hopes, but nope, I'm still me. I might have more projects on my plate than usual, but I'm good at keeping the balls in the air and delegating where I need to. Besides, being in charge probably means I get a staff of some kind, right?"

Idryll muttered, "A staff upside the head, one would hope."

Everyone laughed, and Sinnia asked her, "So, Idryll, do I understand that you joined my daughter after the first *venamisha*?"

The shapeshifter shook her head. "During, actually. There's a test where the *junra* must select from several statues. When she chose the one that looked like me, it brought me there to fight her. Fortunately, at that stage, the object is only to evaluate the *junra*, not to kill them." She bared her teeth. "That comes later."

More laughter. Rayar asked, "So, are you with her all the time then?"

Idryll scowled. "Eww. No. No one can handle that much punishment." Ruby rolled her eyes and returned the napkin in a fast throw at her partner's face. "Besides, she needs time to spend with her boyfriend." She put a salacious emphasis on the last word.

Sinnia perked up. "A boyfriend? Really? Why haven't we met this person?"

Ruby sighed. "Because I want him to like me, maybe? And you all are crazy?"

Morrigan replied, "She's afraid he'll see that she's the least interesting member of the family."

Dralen looked down at his fingernails as if admiring his manicure. "And the least attractive, by far. I can see why she'd want to keep a potential suitor away from us."

Ruby twisted in her seat and poked his nose with a fingertip. "Shut up, you, or your castle will be made entirely of dungeons. Dungeon after dungeon after dungeon. You'll spend a week in each in rotation. One cell will have rats. The next will have centipedes. And so on." She grinned widely. "Hey, you know, I like that idea. Thanks." She swiveled her head to regard Morrigan. "And you, you get to work the floor at the casino for all eternity, serving drinks exclusively to people on losing streaks at the slot machine." They were inevitably the most annoying customers, angry over their losses and trying to make up for it with free beverages.

When she stopped laughing, Sinnia asked, "What about us?"

Ruby nodded. "You two haven't insulted me recently. So, you get a small castle, more a cottage castle, really, somewhere deep in the woods of Oriceran. You'll be permitted to visit us once or twice a year."

Rayar laughed. "If your mother and I have to spend that much time alone together, she'll murder me."

Sinnia nodded primly. "It's true."

Ruby relented. "Okay then, how about we continue as we are and don't worry about all this nonsense until it forces us to?"

Morrigan grinned, the most genuine expression she'd seen from her sister yet. "Deal."

The other members of her family repeated the affirmation until it circled to Idryll. She sighed and shook her head. "Boring. Typical. Honestly, why anyone would put you in charge of anything is beyond me. I wouldn't trust you with a plant-sitting business."

Amid more laughter, the conversation turned to Ruby's truly awful abilities with plants. Somehow, she had the notion that Morrigan had been sharing stories with Idryll and wondered exactly what they filled their time talking about when they were out on patrol. *Oh, a counter alliance, is it? We'll just see about that. My vengeance will be swift and brutal. Like, totally swift and totally brutal. That's definitely how it's going to be. Totally.*

CHAPTER EIGHTEEN

Ruby swirled defensively, using the sword in her right hand to deflect the blade seeking her head, and using the one in the left to convince her second opponent not to press the attack she'd begun a moment before. The clearing was mostly empty for their combat although several villagers had come out to watch. Ruby wasn't sure whether it was because Keshalla was always worth learning from or because Ruby now held a status she'd never had before. Her teacher had suggested it was time to add Idryll to the mix regularly since she would now factor in most, or possibly all, of Ruby's fights.

She had also warned her student that her studies were falling behind. She said, "If you intend to master the double sword, you will have to clear time to practice regularly."

Yeah, like I have time for that sort of thing. Ruby's magic was limited to the force shields covering her blades and what she could pump into her muscles, both by her teacher's orders and by the fact that her hands were both tied up with the weapons. As yet, she still hadn't had time to investigate how to cast magic through her sword. The entities within told her that no one had ever done that with them before, but that was a far cry from saying it was impossible. *Time, time, everything takes time.* She had managed to find the opportunity to spend an hour locking the artifact back into its place, though. That ranked above every other entry on her priority list.

Idryll slammed into her from behind, Keshalla having distracted Ruby at the right moment. The blow came at knee level, knocking her backward over her partner. Her teacher charged forward with a cry, and Ruby used her extra powered muscles to launch herself into a backward roll that carried her to her feet, both swords flicking out to intercept Keshalla's attacks from above and from her right. Her teacher snapped a foot out, but Ruby shifted and caught it on a raised thigh, then smashed that foot out at her teacher. Keshalla blocked down with the pommel of the sword, the two blades scraping down their full length. As they disengaged, Ruby's ankle twisted and erupted into pins and needles.

She jumped back, yelling, "Ouch, jerk," and drew a laugh from her teacher. She sensed rather than saw Idryll off to the side and hopped into a skip kick, landing her heel right in the shapeshifter's stomach. The breath blew out of her foe with a loud gasp, but Ruby didn't have a chance to follow up on the attack since her numbed foot gave out. She controlled her tumble, twisting and writhing to bring her swords to bear in defense again. Keshalla stabbed and kicked from above, and Idryll was close enough that Ruby couldn't get away in that direction.

She was stuck on her back, barely able to defend against

Keshalla's attacks, and would be a sitting duck when her companion did rejoin the fight. Plus, her body ached from head to toe. It was a good feeling, full of confidence that she had come back and was now only tired and exhausted from the extended training session. Still, she was done in. She shouted, "I yield," and let her hands drop to the ground. Her teacher's sword stopped moving an inch from her throat, and Ruby gave her raised eyebrows. "I *said*, I yield. I surrender. I give up. You win. There's no need to be nasty about it."

Keshalla laughed and sheathed her blades with a flourish, then extended a hand to help her up. Idryll grumbled, sounding out of breath, "Wait. Let me hit her a few times before it's over."

Ruby assisted her partner to rise once she'd regained her feet and shook her head. "You're the reason I called it off." Her voice dropped to a stage whisper. "Her I could've taken. But you, no way."

The comment earned her a none too soft kick in the behind, and she straightened in surprise with a laugh. "Oh, I see how it is. Can't handle the truth, huh?" Ruby retrieved her swords and put them back where they belonged, then asked, "I don't suppose you found out anything about the messenger?" She gestured at her house, needing to clean her gear and store it away before her teacher yelled at her for delaying.

Keshalla followed her toward the small home. "I've talked to the elders of all the villages I have connections with, which is most of them. No one remembers anything, or they're not talking. I tend to think it's probably the former at this point since there's no need for them to keep secrets."

Ruby laughed. "Every elderly person I've ever met considers knowledge currency. If you're not willing to offer them something good in trade, their lips are sealed."

Keshalla grinned. "That's a useful piece of wisdom from you, *minari*. I count myself amazed."

Idryll groaned. "Yes, yes, will wonders never cease. Every compliment you give her increases the size of her ego exponentially. You should stop. Maybe switch over to insulting her regularly."

Ruby opened the door and headed into the house. "I think you have that fully covered, Idryll." She pulled the harness that held her swords over her head, hung it on the wall, and started to unlace her boots. "Did Nadar offer anything?"

Keshalla shrugged. "I didn't have a chance to visit with the mystics. It hasn't been that long, you know."

"Slacker. How about we drop in and say hello?"

Word of her impending arrival had preceded her. They arrived at the mystics' home to find them all down on one knee, including Nadar and the archivist. Ruby shook her head and stalked directly over to the pair. Grabbing their hands and pulling them to their feet, she said, "Not just no, but *hell* no. Be nice to me, sure. Feed me the best food and drink, definitely. Give me presents, okay, maybe, if the inclination strikes you. Kneel before me? No way, no how."

Nadar laughed, seeming relieved. She sensed that she

might have passed a test in his eyes. "I'm glad to hear it. One imagined you had not changed, but it's always better to be unnecessarily formal than not formal enough, don't you agree?"

Idryll replied, "I've seen her eat. She definitely does *not* agree."

Ruby snapped out her foot in a kick to the woman's shin and received a slap on the back of her head as a counter. She reached up and rubbed it. "That's it, you get a castle full of dungeons, too." Nadar and Keshalla gave her a confused look, and the archivist laughed at the banter.

The pair of mystics escorted them straight to the archive, where the woman had arranged seats and snacks at her desk. Nadar said, "We don't normally allow food down here, but now that you have completed the *venamisha*, we believe secrecy is essential. Obviously, those before us thought so."

Ruby managed to say around a mouthful of trail bread, with only a small moan of pleasure at the taste, "Sounds like you found some things."

The archivist laughed. "Indeed. The books you brought back from the trial were exceedingly well-chosen."

Keshalla replied smugly, "Of course they were."

Ruby shook her head. "Yeah, you're awesome, and everyone knows it. No need to be snotty about it." She turned her head to the archivist. "What have you discovered?"

The woman unlocked a drawer in her desk and pulled out a tome, setting it flat on the wooden surface. *If she felt the impulse to lock that thing up among the mystics, it must hold something very important.* "This is a journal, written by one of the companions. *Mirra* Mintel's partner."

Idryll said, "Oh, I like that guy."

Ruby replied, "Will you shut up and let the woman speak? Honestly, you're such a chatterbox these days. I think Morrigan is rubbing off on you, and not in a good way." She intercepted the lazy slap Idryll threw her way, and the archivist laughed again at their antics.

The older woman said, "Well, obviously the perspective is a little different since it's from someone on the inside. I won't bore you with talk of the trials and so forth. That's something you can check out whenever you like by visiting us. Without refreshments, of course." She pulled the book slightly away from where their cups of tea rested. "The messenger is discussed near the end. He says they went about their daily lives for 'several weeks' before the messenger appeared. When she did, they were summoned and 'taken away' for an indeterminate amount of time."

Ruby nodded. "That sounds more or less like what I expected, although the idea that someone might take me somewhere for something is a bit of a surprise." She shrugged. "Guess it's pretty much the same old same old, given the process so far." They talked for a while longer, but the mystics shared no more useful information. As they walked out into the open air to look up at the mountain, Keshalla gestured at the pinnacle, which was again mist-covered. "I've been up higher. The castle is invisible."

Ruby replied, "Really? Weird. I figured it would stick around."

Keshalla nodded. "I guess that only you can access it

now, and perhaps others with your permission. Or maybe not."

Ruby laughed. "Well, at least I'll have a place to get away from her." She gestured at Idryll.

Her companion shook her head. "Highly doubtful. Where you go, I go, remember? Kind of the rules."

Ruby sighed. "I'll take this castle. You get the one full of dungeons, identical to Dralen's. Keshalla, you can have one full of random traps and enemies to defeat. Don't thank me. I want you all to be happy. I am a benevolent tyrant." Internally, she laughed. *A custom castle for everyone, this idea keeps getting better all the time.*

CHAPTER NINETEEN

Dieneth gazed down from the balcony onto the floor of his warehouse. It was a new warehouse after the visit from Magic City's vigilantes forced him to abandon the other. It had been worth it, though, to get a sense of them. He knew now that convincing them to join him was a nonstarter, although he had the feeling they might be willing to stay on the sidelines as long as he kept his actions as under the radar as possible. *Probably wishful thinking. Self-styled heroes are rarely logical. Still, one can hope, right?* Below, a gathering of magicals was underway. His trusted people had pulled in their trusted people at his request, and so on a couple of levels down. The final group appeared to be twenty-some strong. *Enough to cause trouble, not enough to bring major heat down on us. It's a tough line to walk, but fortunately, Drow are agile.*

He leapt over the railing and cushioned his fall with a burst of magic, then raised his voice as the gathered assembly turned their eyes to him. He was dressed all in black, soft black jeans over boots, plus a mock turtleneck.

"Thank you for coming. Tonight, we'll strike another blow against the human encroachment onto power and authority that should be ours." There was a small smattering of cheers, and he nodded in appreciation of them. "It's a protracted fight we're in, and tonight won't decide anything. Neither will tomorrow night, or the night after, or the week after. Still, over a long enough timeline, our continuing efforts will resonate and reinforce the next actions. More people will flock to our cause, and the humans will moderate their behavior in response."

Someone he didn't know, a Kilomea with a tall black mohawk, replied, "What if they don't?"

Dieneth grinned. "Well, then, we'll try harder. Because we won't stop until things are the way they ought to be." That incited the crowd to applause, and he nodded again. "All right, let's move."

It would've been an impressive sight, the whole group walking down an industrial street on the southern outskirts of Magic City. However, he'd sent some trusted souls out ahead, and they were defeating the cameras, knocking down drones, and ensuring their progression stayed secret. He broke teams off at intersections, sending friends along with friends to make specific declarations of his displeasure. The first, he ordered to burn down a warehouse that refused to hire non-humans and posted about that policy on social media. He directed the next group to break into a jewelry store another team had failed to get into before. The owner traded in more than human heirlooms, taking advantage of magicals who were down on their luck and offering them pennies on the dollar. He dispatched others off to similar things, all with the admonition that they shouldn't take action until the clock hit midnight. Ten minutes before that mark, he and his two most trusted lieutenants arrived at Hazard, a human-only club about halfway toward the Strip.

There was no signage to indicate it was human-only, of course. Still, the street knew, and when a pair of Kilomea dared to venture inside, they wound up getting attacked by a human gang as soon as they were off the premises. The Kilomea gave as good as they got, and the fight finished with only bumps and bruises for the magicals. However, it wasn't the attack's result that was important, but rather the emboldened attitude that caused it to happen in the first place.

Before entering, they sheathed themselves in disguises, dressed like and appearing as average tourists out on the town. Drunk humans filled the bar, so they avoided it entirely and instead made a careful circuit, avoiding physical contact that could reveal their disguise while identifying all the security guards they might have to face. They finally stopped at a high-top in a corner that was momentarily empty, and he leaned over toward them. They mimicked his posture, and he cautioned, "Remember, killing is not an option, not even by accident. It will draw down too much heat on us, and we're not ready for that quite yet." He had killed the gang members in the alley, but that was more as a way to give notice to the humans in the city that magicals wouldn't tolerate their actions any longer. Since then, his operations had been nonlethal. Even if they hadn't been restraining themselves, this was too many people. Death on that scale would bring in all sorts of authorities from the outside, possibly including bounty hunters from Vegas, who he had no desire to tangle with.

They nodded. "Broken bones only. We'll stay away from the heads."

"Excellent. Let's do it." Their disguises vanished as they reached down and pulled combat sticks from thigh sheaths. The patrons at the nearest table only realized that something weird was happening when the wooden weapons slammed into legs and arms, snapping them with a loud *crunch*. The place erupted in screams and confusion, with people pushing instinctively toward the exits. "Dammit," he said, "the cattle are going to kill themselves if they're not careful." Dieneth pointed at one of his lieutenants and ordered, "Fly over and make sure the front doors are open so they don't get crushed." She obeyed immediately, and he turned to the other. "Do the same with the back door. Then, give the humans some more pain."

He waded into the nearest, striking only hard enough to create bruises and fear, worried that if they wound up on the floor, they'd get trampled. *I should have expected them to react like sheep. I won't make that mistake again.* The security guards had realized what was up, and several deployed toward the doors to help people escape. A couple decided to challenge him instead, lifting bright yellow tasers to point them in his direction. He asked, "Really?"

They both pulled the triggers, and he used force magic with a wave of his hand to knock the darts into the floor. He stepped forward and slammed his stick into the leg of the one on the right, then smashed an elbow into the ribs of the other. The first went down, and the second cringed.

He swept a foot around to take the upright one's legs out from underneath him, and his head slammed off the floor as he landed. Dieneth didn't think it would've been hard enough to kill him, but he certainly couldn't be sure. *Well, ultimately what will be, will be.*

He shook his head at the security guards now trying to escape along with the patrons. "Oh no, you don't. You've chosen to defend this place actively and taken payment from it. You're going down." He strode toward the entrance and his targets, throwing blasts of force magic around to destroy bottles behind the bar, to shatter the electronics in the DJ booth, and generally create havoc and property damage. He laughed out loud. "Man, I love my job."

Ruby was in Alejo's backyard on the evening of the following day. She used illusion to coat herself, so this time she could accept a beer bottle from the other woman, and they drank together. Ruby said, "You know, this is how friendships usually start."

Alejo snorted. "With one person in disguise so the other person doesn't know who they really are?"

She shook her head. "No, that's totally more a romantic relationship kind of thing." The sheriff laughed. "I meant having a drink, sharing information, talking. Like normal people."

Alejo chuckled. "Neither of us is normal, but I get what you're saying. I presume the incident at Hazard was the sort of thing you warned me about the last time we met?"

"Yeah. Drow male, don't know much more about him, except he's a jerk who thinks humans have overstepped."

The other woman replied, "Right. We've been watching for him ever since you sent the email with the additional information. Too bad we didn't find him before last night. At least no one was killed. Hospitals are busy today, though."

Ruby frowned. She hadn't sent an email, so it must've been Demetrius. After a moment, she let her initial annoyance go. *What did I think he would do, stand idly by and not help out where he can? I'd never date someone who would act like that. Besides, I didn't forbid it, and clearly, the sharing had some benefit. Maybe I need to stop being such a control freak.*

The sheriff asked, "What do you think we should do about him and his people?"

Ruby shrugged. "Keep your eyes open, and if you see something developing, email or call me. If you can't get me, for whatever reason, call Andrews."

Alejo coughed on her drink, then wiped her mouth. "You, recommending I work with the PDA? Do you really believe this guy is that bad?"

Ruby nodded. "I think he has a message that will resonate. I think some of what he says makes sense, but he's also convinced me that he'd burn down the city to prove his point. Just because I'm sympathetic to a couple of ideas doesn't mean I will accept the fact that his tactics cross the line."

The sheriff straightened slightly and nodded. "I'm glad to hear you still have a line."

Ruby laughed. "Not going to lie, it's a little hard to see sometimes, but it's there. No bodies, minimal property damage where we can, and focus on keeping innocent people safe."

The other woman grinned. "Sounds reasonable to me." She gestured with her empty bottle. "Another drink, and maybe some talk about something other than work?"

Ruby laughed. "Sure. Be careful, though. You might be risking the development of a potential friendship."

CHAPTER TWENTY

The atmosphere in the small palace at the center of the kemana felt dour to Ruby. Her father escorted her through the main doors, and guards stood at posts where there had been none during her last visit, a testament to the increased strain caused underneath Magic City by the events above. That demeanor continued in the Council chamber itself, where those seated around the round table wore expressions signaling stress and in some cases, outright displeasure. *The Drow looks like she's ready to stab someone.* The only exception was the dwarf, Grentham, whose neutral expression nonetheless managed to come off somehow smug. *There's something off about that dude. He bears looking into. I need to talk to Alejo about him.*

The leader of the group, Lord Maldren, rapped his knuckles on the table for attention. Side conversation stopped, and he announced, "Our first order of business is the events surrounding Worldspan Security."

Elnyier replied, "I have spoken with them since the unfortunate incident at their building. They say it was nothing, a gas leak, and that they lost no personnel. Some injuries, as you'd expect."

Ruby stilled the impulse to shake her head. In their conversation, Alejo had mentioned the explosion, and the information she provided didn't quite match up with the Drow's story. *Or, more specifically, I guess the security company's story. I suppose that if someone did take action against them, they'd want to keep that quiet.* The sheriff didn't have confirmation of anything, only suspicions, so it wasn't worth bringing up.

In a neutral tone, Grentham said, "My company still stands ready to handle your needs. Just let us know. Councilmember discount."

Maldren replied, "Thank you, Grentham, as always. Now, our second item on the agenda is the Paranormal Defense Agency." Subtle displeasure turned into outright hostility on several faces. *I guess it's not only me who thinks Andrews is a scumbag.* Andirelle, the witch, said, "Their drones are everywhere. I'm starting to feel downright hunted. Or haunted, maybe."

Bartrak, the Kilomea, replied, "We have tracked their patterns and made a thorough accounting of all the aerial vehicles in the area. There is a surveillance net stretching from the mountains to the north to the city's edges to the south. The actual devices differ in size, but when you plot them all, the pattern is clear."

The gnome Challen, one of the people Ruby liked best in the Kemana, remarked, "Good work, my friend. That is useful information to have." The Kilomea nodded, and the dichotomy of the smallest sized person in the room and the largest one being friendly struck Ruby. *Or maybe friends for real. Who knows? No weirder than Alejo and me chatting over beers.*

Grentham grunted. "One of my people up above has a strong suspicion that the PDA is using autonomous vehicles for surveillance as well. Perhaps you should add that to the next version of your plot, Bartrak."

The Kilomea looked thoughtful. "That might explain some gaps that seemed like they shouldn't be there. Thank you for the information."

Ruby couldn't stop the corners of her mouth from turning down. *That had to come from Prex. Why would he do that?* A moment later, logic kicked in to combat the emotional response. *Of course, he would do that. News has to flow up to the Council, and as far as he knows, I'm not a member. Just probie twenty-three. He's doing his best to protect the people in Magic City, as we all are.*

Maldren asked, "Any other thoughts on the Paranormal Defense Agency?" A growl or two sounded in response, but nothing substantive. The weary-looking Mist Elf nodded. "Very well. Our third order of business is the unexpected increase in the number of fires and property crimes in the city. Doubtless you've noticed that Rayar's daughter is with us. She has some information to share on that topic."

Ruby, who had been standing behind her father's chair, stepped slightly away so she would be clearly in everyone's view. "I struck up a friendly connection with Sheriff Alejo a while back. One of those random things. Anyway, sometimes she talks about work, and when she mentioned something about the fires, I asked if I could share the information." Nods encouraged her to continue. "The chiefs at the fire departments who responded to the scenes, most specifically the plastics factory but also several others, believe someone set them intentionally."

A ripple of anger flowed through the Council. Elnyier snapped, "Evidence?"

How about an anti-human Drow, for starters? For the moment, Ruby figured that the Drow male behind the antihuman efforts was working alone, but she had a suspicion he'd find a sympathetic ear in his species representative on the Council. Since she didn't know that particular event was his doing with a hundred percent certainty, she wasn't going to bring him up. "The fires burned hotter than they should have, and they didn't find any accelerants."

Grentham snorted. "Which means that perhaps they're not doing a good job of finding it. I get it. Magic is the simplest solution, Occam's Razor, and all that. It's far from being proof."

Ruby shrugged. "Sheriff Alejo feels the same way, that more investigation is required. Nonetheless, the fact that they were most likely arson and that property crimes against human-owned businesses have kicked up a notable amount seemed relevant to bring to the Council's attention. Thank you for your time." She delivered the last with a bit of a growl and bowed her head respectfully to cover it. *Down, Ruby. No one likes having their beliefs challenged, no matter what planet they're from.*

Bartrak nodded slowly. "I will ask my people to keep an eye out. Humans make up a significant portion of our customers, and this is bad for business, if true." The others made noises to do the same, but for a few, it seemed to be only lip service. *Yeah, Elnyier, Grentham, Rosalind, I'm watching you.*

Andrielle, the Atlantean representative, said, "It might be worth seeing if similar things are happening in other cities that house a kemana. I will reach out to my people across the country."

Maldren thanked her, then asked, "Any other discussion of this topic?"

None arrived, and he started to move on to the next item. Elnyier interrupted him, rising suddenly from her seat and causing everyone at the table to look at her. She intoned, "Lord Maldren. Over the last many years, you have led us capably through the growth of Magic City, delivering prosperity and maintaining a comfortable balance among our different groups. We applaud you for that." What seemed like a compliment was colored by the sense that something with an edge was coming. "However, your style is inadequate to the present time. We need a leader with more vision, one who is more action-oriented, let's say. You are clearly *not* that person. I nominate myself to take the leadership in your place."

The room was dead silent, and Maldren was still for several seconds. Ruby recognized the blank look on his face, similar to the one she used when she didn't want to express her emotions to others. He finally replied, "Very well. We have rules for this, and such a challenge is in keeping with them. I do not voluntarily resign from the position so we will vote. Are there any other nominations?"

Anders, the wizard, said, "I nominate my wife,

Rosalind." The woman in question smiled broadly and nodded to accept.

Maldren said, "Very well. Any others?"

Ruby leaned into her father's ear and whispered, "You should volunteer," but he shook his head and remained silent.

Maldren said, "Challen, please distribute the stones." Ruby deduced that the gnome held some official position that required him to bring said stones because he produced a brown suede pouch that held polished rocks in ten different colors, each about the size of the top section of her thumb. Maldren was assigned yellow, Elnyier black, and Rosalind blue. Each member of the Council received one of each color. They passed the bag around the room, once emptied of the other rocks, and when it made its way back to Challen, he pulled the stones out one by one to count votes.

Elnyier won and accepted congratulations from the others. Ruby bent to ask her father a question, but he shushed her. They said their goodbyes and exited the palace, which would soon become the Drow woman's home. When they were far enough away that no one would overhear, Rayar explained, "Elnyier wouldn't have pushed the issue unless she already had the votes. Rosalind throwing her name in might've been random, not part of the plan, or it might have been intentional misdirection. In either case, she would've been a worse choice than Elnyier."

Ruby, thinking about the Drow connection to the anti-human efforts in Ely, shook her head. "I hope you're right." *I really don't think you are.*

CHAPTER TWENTY-ONE

Ruby arrived at Margrave's door twenty minutes before their scheduled meeting time, knowing both that he'd be ready for her and that Daphne would show up ten minutes early because that's how she was. He opened it with a smile, and she said, "I wanted to discuss a couple of things before our friendly neighborhood potion maker arrives."

He laughed. "Perfect. Tea is still brewing, but the cookies just came out of the oven."

She shook her head. "I don't understand how you find time to bake."

"Everyone needs a hobby. Besides, I come up with some of my most creative ideas while my conscious brain focuses on baking."

Ruby helped him carry the tray full of baked goods down to the workshop and sat at a diagonal from him in her usual spot. "First, I wondered if you could build a container for my belt to hold reloads for the dart gun."

He frowned. "Are you really in situations where you need more than five doses?"

She made a noise somewhere between a sigh and a groan. *Yeah, this gig is more challenging than anyone thought it could be.* "I didn't think I would be back when we talked about it at first, but it turns out more would be better."

He shook his head. "I won't ask because I don't want to be any more frightened for you than I already am. I can work on that. It'll take a few days." He slid a set of five darts over to her. "I figured you might need more after I heard about something involving a religious commune that was illegally selling magic items."

Ruby accepted them and nodded. "Ran into a weird thing during that particular adventure. The folks I was with have really good tech, like, top of the line, and yet somehow their comms were jammed during it. I wondered if it could have been magical rather than technological."

Margrave tapped a fingernail on his teeth as he thought. After several seconds, he shrugged. "Sure, probably. I have to look into it, but offhand I can imagine some possibilities. Interfering with the electromagnetic makeup of the area might work, for instance."

Ruby raised a hand. "Now you're way over my head. Think about it and let me know what you find out."

He laughed. "Will do. Any other interesting news to share?"

She drew a deep breath since it was still weird to talk about. "Remember that time I almost passed out, and you got to see Idryll's true nature?"

He nodded. "Vividly."

"I finished that process. The *venamisha*. Three rounds."

"And?"

She didn't for a moment think that he hadn't already done research into the topic, so the question made her grin. "When I'm in charge, things are going to be different."

He laughed. "I'll believe it when I see it, sunshine. In the meantime, go let Daphne in."

The doorbell rang an instant later, and Ruby shook her head. "Between tech and talent, you have it all, my friend."

She let the witch in and shared hugs with her, then rushed to catch up as Daphne bounded down the staircase into the workshop. As soon as her roommate reached Margrave, she blurted, "I think I've nailed it. The distribution system."

He grinned. "Well, sit, and tell me all about it." While they conferred, Ruby unpacked her backpack, which contained one of the large model drones she was using to watch over the house. She had three of them in rotation, and Demetrius had refined the artificial intelligence that monitored them to the point that they could now differentiate between humanoids and everything else. It was a significant step forward since the night they'd been shaken out of bed because an enormous raccoon had stood on its hind legs and set off a full-scale alert.

She opened a canister filled with jacks, children's toys serving as a substitute for caltrops to experiment with release mechanisms. Rath had been right, it *was* a good idea, and she was starting to get a handle on how she had to do it. She'd initially tried a single hinged compartment, but the panel didn't fall away fast enough to avoid impacting the dispersal of the individual pieces. So now she was testing a pair of hinged covers that fell open simultaneously. She had a hunch it would work but might require positioning the caltrops differently within, maybe with some sort of spacers.

Her first idea of jamming them all in and letting gravity sort them out proved unworkable when the whole bunch fell out in a couple of large clumps. If it wouldn't work any other way, she'd accept that and hope they dispersed upon impact, but it wasn't what she wanted. She envisioned a smooth stream of spiked objects flying out behind a drone. If she had any real free time, she'd devise a mechanism to eject them from the rear one by one, but she'd put that on the innovation list rather than the initial design plan.

After an hour, Margrave and Daphne had their project figured out. It was a patch with a potion capsule embedded in it. Smashing the capsule spread the liquid through the patch, which leeched into the skin over a wide area, ensuring fast absorption. The whole thing was about the size of her palm and looked incredibly simple, now that it was right there on the table. She had no doubt it had taken a great deal of effort to get that far, no matter how obvious it seemed upon completion. She said, "You know, that's going to have a real market among the wealthy. Emergency healing only a hand slap away? They'll be all over it. How long does it last?"

Daphne's grin covered her entire face. "The adhesive works for a couple of days, so it depends on whether you wanted to change it every day or let it rest until it starts to wear off. Your average person probably wouldn't want to pay for a daily replacement. If you're right, and it has a market among the wealthy, I bet they could."

Margrave said, "This calls for a drink. Daphne, go get the decanter and the glasses that are in that cabinet on the far end of the room."

While the witch was gone, he slipped Ruby another EMP and whispered, "These things are expensive. Don't use them willy-nilly." When Daphne returned, and they all had a partially filled glass, they raised a toast to her success.

Ruby said, "Okay, total change of subject. At the Council meeting, one member mentioned that the Paranormal Defense Agency could be using autonomous vehicles as surveillance devices. Using the cameras, maybe, collecting data on the occupants and where they go, that sort of thing. A friend of mine said they might even have the legal right to do it, depending on the policies around self-driving vehicles. I'm going to be honest. I'm really uncomfortable with the whole idea. Anything you two can think of to mess with it?"

Daphne laughed. "Ruby the Crusader."

She nodded. "Truth, justice, and the right to gamble. I'm all about it."

Her roommate said, "They must be collecting the information wirelessly, right? I'm sure they're not sending agents to download data from the cars."

Ruby replied, "Fair guess."

Daphne shrugged. "Then some sort of jammer on the car to prevent the collection would likely work."

"Getting them onto all the cars would take a lot of effort. I'm probably not that much of a crusader." *Maybe Morrigan and Idryll could do it during their patrols, or perhaps I can get the Desert Ghosts to help out. I bet they'd be into that.*

Margrave said, "You know, the magical signature that those vehicles emit is unique. I read something about it the other day. It might be possible to create tiny pods that would home in on them. We'd miss the older ones that were technology only, but at this point, there's likely not too many of them still rolling."

Ruby nodded. "You're thinking drone release?"

"Exactly, probably from pretty high up. In order to make them small enough, we wouldn't want them to have engines, only steering. They'd be just jamming, flight, and detection." His face brightened. "Heck, we could discard the detection and flight pieces after the thing made contact so they'd be even less likely to be noticed."

Ruby grinned at his enthusiasm. "Uh-oh. I think you have a new obsession."

Margrave laughed. "Could be. That'll be my next project. A little nonviolent resistance sounds like fun." He sobered suddenly. "Wait, no, dammit. The jamming might mess with the actual driving, which probably uses a wireless component as well."

She frowned, unwilling to let the idea go. "What if I got you one of the communication devices they're using to transmit? Do you think you could customize it?"

Daphne interrupted, "Where would you get one of those?"

Ruby scowled at her playfully. "I have friends."

The witch shook her head with a smile. "You do not. You're too busy for friends."

She countered, "*You're* my friends. The best friendships are both work and pleasure, right?" Daphne opened her mouth to reply, and Ruby said, "Shut up. So, Margrave, what do you think?"

He laughed. "Get me a transmitter, and I'll see what I can do."

CHAPTER TWENTY-TWO

Ruby closed her locker, having changed into the black base layer of her uniform, each part of the process calming her mind a little more. The stone floor was cold on her bare feet. She pulled her sword from its sheath and left the carrier behind as well, taking the naked blade into her meditation space. She bolted the door, then called up the warding magic of the golden outer ring, which activated with a shimmer and a *hum* that was more sensed than heard.

The world quieted as it always did when the protection rose as if it had banished the invisible pressures working upon her. She let her arms hang at her sides and closed her eyes, focusing her mind inward, taking all the extraneous thoughts and concerns and packing them away for the moment. Even though she'd explicitly designed this chamber to deal with the Atlantean inside her, she had found it useful for any situation that required deep concentration.

She'd never used it for anything other than meditation

before, so today's experiment was something new. She extended the blade and turned in a circle, noting precisely how far it could extend outward to avoid crossing the ward. *As long as I don't lunge, I'll be fine.* Upward was no problem, assuming she didn't stretch too far in that direction. Part of her training guidelines with Keshalla had always been adapting her style to the surrounding conditions, so this wouldn't be an unfamiliar task. Plus, it would allow her to practice moves that she might not otherwise do in a more wide-open space.

She opened her eyes, keeping them soft and defocused. An imagined opponent appeared before her, holding a sword similar to hers but longer and slightly more curved to fit their greater height. For some reason, her virtual opponents were almost always taller than she was. *A therapist would probably have fun with that.* She pushed the thought away and raised the dull side of her blade to her forehead in a salute that her rival immediately copied.

She stepped slowly back, concentrating on each part of the motion, ensuring her form was perfect. Simultaneously, she began to build her magic reserves, readying power for use. It would make only a small time difference in employing it but might add intensity to her attacks. *Optimization is what practice is all about.*

What followed next was more an intricate ballet than it was combat. She moved as slowly as she was capable of, feeling the interplay of each muscle as she brought her sword up to intercept an imagined downward strike at the perfect angle. As the blades clashed in her mind, she shifted her weight to perform a riposte, sliding her weapon along the other blade and twisting it so the edge pointed in the right direction. Her fictional opponent was skilled and leaned back far enough to let her sword pass in front of him.

She repositioned her feet in perfect balance to address his next attack. The practice went on like that, ultra-slow-motion, a complete focus on muscles and movement until suddenly she slipped into the inner space occupied by the duo of entities inside her weapon. She was fully aware of her body continuing to move but realized she had somehow segmented a part of her mind to achieve this commune.

Shalia, the female inhabitant of her artifact weapon, smiled. "You are becoming far more adept at partitioning your focus without sacrificing anything. Well done."

Instead of Ruby's preferred location, they were in the other woman's, with waves lapping off to her left and warm sand sneaking in between her toes. The sun felt lovely. She grinned and replied, "I guess I have one thing to thank the Atlantean bastard in my head for, anyway."

Tyrsh, the male inhabitant, commented, "Splintering your mind is a key element to proper use of the sword. If you are in contact with us while you fight, we will be better able to help you, rather than trying to push our way into your consciousness in times of stress."

Logical. "How did you get into the sword, anyway?" She'd often wondered. Shalia replied, "It defeated us, and instead of dissipating or heading into whatever lies beyond this world, somehow we wound up here."

"The same for both of you?"

Tyrsh confirmed it. "Yes, the same."

Ruby frowned, thinking that being sucked inside involuntarily didn't sound like a very fine gig. "Did it get both of you at the same time? I mean, in the same battle?"

Shalia replied, "Definitely not. I have been here far longer. Surely you can sense that in my comparative maturity."

Her companion—*Sword mate? Roommate?*—gave the other woman a plastic smile and enthused sarcastically, "Love you too, darling." Shalia laughed.

Imagine being trapped for eternity with someone you didn't choose. Ruby shuddered. "Is there a way for me to cast spells through the sword or absorb them with it?" She congratulated herself for finally remembering to ask.

Shalia shook her head. "No, such things are not possible."

Tyrsh contradicted her. "I'm afraid that, as usual, you're incorrect. Maybe in the ancient times *you* come from that was true, but it's possible with appropriate training. She's already begun it by learning to separate parts of her mind." The two argued back and forth about it until he finally shrugged. "Clearly, it was after your time. But it's entirely possible."

A new voice joined the conversation. "It definitely is." A vertical tear appeared in midair, and the Atlantean representing the Rhazdon artifact in her arm stepped through it, looking for all the world like he was walking down a flight of invisible stairs until his feet hit the sand. "If it is your wish, I can help you along the path to achieving it."

Ruby crossed her arms and frowned at him. "Out of the goodness of your heart, I presume?"

He laughed, his striking features and heavy black braids a marked comparison to the suddenly plain-looking inhabitants of her sword. They were beautiful and handsome, respectively, but the Atlantean was downright stunning. *Evil is always seductive, so they say.* "Of course not. The more power you gain, the better it will be for me when you finally realize a partnership between us is your destiny."

Shalia shook her head. "You know you can't trust him. Even his ulterior motives have ulterior motives behind them."

Ruby laughed. "It's turtles all the way down. I get it. But, truth be told, as long as I'm stuck with the damn artifact, I should try to make the best of it." She shifted her attention back to the Atlantean. "How can I be confident this isn't an effort to manipulate me?"

He shrugged. "Remember, this is your place. Well, at the moment, yours influenced by them, but ultimately your mind controls all here. If you would find it reassuring, there is absolutely no reason they cannot be present for any teaching and training we undertake together."

Ruby turned to the inhabitants of her sword. "I don't understand the rules of this place particularly well. Do you have any power over him?"

They both shook their heads, and Tyrsh replied, "As he says, all the power here is yours. We can all make suggestions, attempt to influence you in ways both obvious and less so, but ultimately unless you allow it, we cannot subvert your will."

Ruby frowned. "Unless I allow it?"

Shalia nodded. "In the past, when paired with a weaker fighter, the wielder has chosen to permit us to rise and inhabit their body during combat. It has allowed some to survive when they otherwise would not have."

"You didn't mention this to me why?"

Tyrsh laughed. "Any number of reasons. First, your personality is not the type to take kindly to the idea of losing control. Second, you are entirely adequate as a fighter, which means our occasional advice is enough unless you wish to have a deeper integration. Finally, once he joined us," he gestured at the Atlantean, "it didn't make sense to do anything that might weaken your mental barriers."

She nodded. "Good thinking, but I prefer to make my own choices. In the future, if such options exist, tell me." They bowed their heads in assent, looking chagrined. She turned her gaze on the smiling Atlantean. "And you, gleeful boy, don't get excited. I trust them about thirty million times more than I trust you. Explain to me how I need to change to use my sword that way."

He replied, "Currently you think of the sword as a tool, a weapon to be wielded. This is, of course, completely logical and normal. However, if you want to use it to channel power, it will need to become a part of you. Surely you've noticed that wizards are rarely without their wands, even if they're not using them at the moment. It's more than the need to have it at hand if they wish to use magic. The constant bond is essential to using it as a repository and tool for your magic. You will need to become as close to your sword as a wizard or witch is to their wand."

She frowned. "Why isn't that the case with my magic dagger?"

He shrugged. "Different magic went into its creation, so it operates by different rules. By definition, if you can use it for that purpose, it doesn't require the same sort of bond you would need for your sword."

"How do you know so much about this?"

"I am fundamentally magic. Unlike the other two, who were beings who transitioned into an object, my very nature straddles the physical and magical world. As such, I have knowledge and insights that others lack."

Ruby scowled at his arrogant tone. "Well, if you weren't a total power-hungry douchebag, that would make you a pretty valuable resource for magic research. Of course, I can't trust you, so that's out."

He shrugged. "You will feel about me how you will feel, but the truth is you can trust me to the degree that our objectives are aligned. We both wish to increase your power, so rest assured I will always be on your side to reach that goal."

Tyrsh laughed. "Plus, you'll always look for an opportunity to take her over."

The Atlantean inclined his head toward the other man. "It is my nature."

Ruby said, "Okay, I'll think about it, now go away." He obliged, vanishing. She asked, "Is he truly gone?"

Shalia replied, "He is."

"Thank goodness. There's one more thing I need to talk to you about. I've chosen a name for the sword, and I wanted to be sure you approved. I chose it because of a few different things, but primarily because I think of you both as benevolent spirits within the weapon, and my family's casino happens to be named Spirits."

Tyrsh drawled, "Let me guess. The sword's name is Spirit."

Ruby laughed. "No, I'm not that uncreative. The sword's name is Eidolon."

Shalia repeated the name as if testing it out and smiled. "Clever and elegant. I love it."

Tyrsh nodded. "Completely acceptable."

Ruby grinned. "Eidolon it is, then."

CHAPTER TWENTY-THREE

Ruby finished putting on her makeup, tossed her brushes back in their jar, and arranged her hair in Harley Quinn-style ponytails. Demetrius had promised to take her out on a date some time before. He'd sprung on her at the last minute that today was the day they were going out to lunch together. It hadn't left her a lot of time to get ready, but then again, she wasn't all that high maintenance in the first place.

She pulled a sundress over her head, made sure it settled properly and slipped on a pair of strappy sandals that wrapped around her ankle. The dress was pale blue with darker designs, the footwear a light leather somewhere between sand-colored and tan. Her shield pendant was on display, and she slid on the cuffs that created magical shields when struck together.

She descended the stairs from the attic and made her way to his room. The door opened before she could knock. He wore a preppy-looking outfit of a collared shirt and cargo shorts with sandals and looked fantastic. She told him so, and he grinned and replied, "You're far too kind. Our ride's outside. Let's go."

Their conveyance turned out to be an autonomous vehicle, and Ruby hid her scowl at the sight of it. She made a mental note to call Prex since she'd forgotten to do so and get the transmission device. *If he doesn't have it anymore, maybe we'll jack another car and take it.* They rode to a place in the southeast of the city, one of the original neighborhoods from before the casinos, full of tall, narrow buildings and street-level shops with colorful awnings.

The car dropped them off in front of an otherwise undistinguished house, and he led the way to a basement door. He pushed it open and held it for her, and Ruby was surprised to see a restaurant inside, especially since there were no markings on the exterior to indicate it was there. Four-top linoleum tables and beat-up chairs filled the main area, with a counter blocking access to the back. The walls were cracking but painted a joyful shade of yellow. It was immediately homey, as if they'd walked into someone's dining room.

A dark-skinned man, probably in his sixties with a bald head and a white goatee, grinned at their arrival from his position behind the counter beside an old cash register. "Sit anywhere. I'll be over with menus in a minute." Demetrius led her to a table and pulled out a chair for her. She laughed and sat, then he tucked it in and took his.

Ruby teased, "You're such a gentleman, at least when people are watching. This place is a surprise. How did you know it was here?"

He leaned back with a smile and spread his arms wide.

"This is my old neighborhood. Everyone who lives here knows where to get the best barbecue."

She licked her lips. "I thought that was what I smelled, and I'm glad to hear it's true. But I can't imagine how a place this small stays in business."

He shrugged. "Well, I'm not a restauranteur myself, but I do know the owners spend most of their time running a food truck. This is mainly to keep their hand in when the county fair season is past, or on weekends without gigs, or whatever. Doesn't change the fact that it's some of the most amazing barbecue you'll find anywhere."

The man came back with menus and grinned down at Ruby. "I can tell this is your first time here. Not too impressive, I know."

She shook her head. "On the contrary, this place is great. I don't think I need to look at a menu. I'll trust you to choose for me."

Their server laughed and said, "Now that is a smart decision. Same for you, boy?"

Demetrius didn't seem to mind the familiarity. *Probably he knows the owners since they're from the neighborhood.* "Perfect. Make it so."

The other man rolled his eyes. "Jean-Luc Picard, you're not." Her boyfriend laughed at his back as he departed.

Ruby asked, "Are the insults free, or do they charge extra?"

Her date shook his head with a smile. "Everyone gets treated like family, which is to say that they pull no punches." Their conversation stilled as a couple more people came in and took tables.

Demetrius exchanged nods with them, and Ruby asked, "So, do you know everyone here, or what?"

"I've spent a decent amount of time in this restaurant. I'm a big fan of barbecue. So, I've gotten to meet most of the regulars. In this place, pretty much everyone is a regular. You either know about it and love it, or you're completely unaware. It's rare that someone new walks in off the street."

Ruby chuckled. "Yeah, the complete lack of signage or indication that a restaurant exists here would do that."

"Right?"

"So, is everything okay? Your gigs are going well, that sort of thing?" It occurred to her that she hadn't spent much time with him recently, given how caught up she was in other responsibilities. *Yeah, you have the makings of a great girlfriend, Ruby. Probably invited you out to break up with you.*

He nodded. "Some of the work I've done for you has taught me things I can use with other clients, so that's all to the good. Plus, some of the other casinos we made contact with have thrown a little work my way. Low-level stuff, obviously. They don't want me in their systems. Still, it all adds up to a decent business."

"Is it what you want to do?"

He nodded. "It's exactly what I want to do. Using my magic and my brain together makes me happier than any other job I've had. I mean, it's still work. I have no desire to fill all my waking hours with it. Man cannot live on work alone. Sometimes video games are needed, too."

She chuckled. "Or occasional dates, right?"

"Very occasionally," he responded dryly. When she

flinched, he laughed. "I'm only screwing with you, Ruby. We both do what we can, and we're both busy people. We don't have to be in a rush."

Food arrived a moment later, an empty plate for each of them and three family-style plates set in the middle of the table. The server said, "Just realized I didn't give you my name. I'm Dutch. Anyway, what we've got here are some ribs, some pulled pork, some pulled chicken, some baked beans, cornbread, a little fresh bread out of the oven, some corn, and if you're still hungry afterward, there's some strawberry shortcake in the back."

The smells were heaven, and the food tasted equally good when they dug in. While they ate, they didn't talk about much besides great meals they'd eaten, how this barbecue stacked up against others, and so on. By the time they finished, Ruby was well and truly stuffed. She told Dutch, "I'll have to take a rain check on the strawberry shortcake."

The man nodded. "Does that mean you'll come back around sometime?"

Ruby smiled up at him. "Definitely, assuming I can get this big lug to take me out on another date."

Dutch grinned at Demetrius. "Your mother raised you better than that, boy."

It clicked in her head an instant before Demetrius said, "Lay off, Dad. So, what do you think?"

An older woman, similar to her husband except the gray hair was on her scalp rather than her face, wandered up beside him. "From what Dutch said, she's wonderful. Hi dear, I'm Claire."

Ruby replied, "I've heard so much about you both,

except apparently your names and what you do." She kicked Demetrius under the table, and his yelp earned a laugh from both of his parents. "It's very nice to meet you."

His mother said, "We've heard a lot about you too, all of it good. Hopefully, our little ruse didn't offend you."

Ruby shook her head. "Not at all. Although I'm a big believer in revenge." She scowled dramatically at Demetrius, and everyone laughed again.

Dutch ordered, "Bring her back soon, boy."

Demetrius stood and extended a hand to help her up. "I will, Dad, if she'll make time for me."

Claire said, "Hopefully you realize what a fine man you're with, Ruby."

"I definitely do, ma'am." They exited and walked the dozen blocks up to the Strip, then sauntered along it. Eventually, the conversation turned serious.

Demetrius said, "Now that you've completed the *venamisha*, your future's probably going to be pretty complicated, huh?"

Ruby nodded. "Whoever's with me will have to deal with Idryll, for one. She's a forever problem."

Demetrius laughed. "I'm telling her you said that."

"Don't you dare. Plus, I'll probably have to spend a lot of time on Oriceran, which means that anyone who wants to be with me will doubtless be bouncing back and forth between the planets."

He shrugged. "With portals, it's not a bad commute or anything. Not a deal-breaker."

Ruby added, "Probably have to cope with additional security and training, too. I guess I'll be some kind of public figure, with all the challenges that involves."

He stopped and pulled gently on her arm to make her face him. "I'm still not running away."

Ruby looked into his eyes. "Hardest part, he'd have to put up with me."

He kissed her and gave a serious nod. "Now that you mention that, maybe I ought to rethink this."

She smacked him, and he laughed. Grabbing his hand, she pulled him with a purpose toward one side of the Strip. He asked, "Wait, what are you doing?"

She called over her shoulder, "We're heading to Spirits. If you're going to make me meet your parents without any warning, it seems only fair that I return the favor."

CHAPTER TWENTY-FOUR

Jared walked behind the convoy of large crates and cases that rolled from the loading dock through the back areas of Invention casino. They'd decided not to take their normal couple of weeks to research the casino before physically moving into the space. Instead, they were on the ground the day after the ink was dry on the contract. Grentham had urged, and he'd agreed, that they needed the money to flow as quickly as possible since they would have to add personnel to handle this gig and the ones that would doubtless follow.

He spotted small camera domes in the ceiling, which he heartily approved of. He felt equally strongly in the opposite direction about the lack of guards in the hallways. Loading docks were always a potential vulnerability and needed careful oversight. *We have a lot to offer these folks in the realm of security, that's for sure. I get why they probably wanted to do it themselves, but that wasn't a great choice.*

The crates turned, and he followed them into one of the four rooms allotted to them. The central area, with a door on each wall, was a small kitchen. His people had pushed the tables and chairs out of the way so they could get their equipment through. On the left was a locker room, and huge containers full of gear for his team, including uniforms, suits, weapons, medical stuff, you name it, went in there. The equipment was all part of a remote security setup they'd used any number of times in the past, one that allowed them to deploy to the field and work out of any location easily. It would serve as a good bridge between Day One and when they got the place appropriately outfitted.

The room in the back would house the security station. More crates went in there, and once they removed the fronts would have displays, controls, communication gear, and the like. A team of gnomes was already in the room, pulling wires through the ceilings to provide them with proper connections to the existing security infrastructure. The casino owners hadn't wanted to rely entirely on them, so they were reserving the existing security center for their use. That was fine with Jared, who preferred to use his setup, anyway.

As soon as it was uncrated and connected, they would have twenty-four-seven surveillance going on the public-access floors, which was the first step in the right direction. Once they completed the move-in, several movers would shed their overalls for suits and uniforms and get to work patrolling the place. It would be an ad hoc arrangement for a while, but it should be adequate for any problems that might arise. *As long as no one tries to blow up the casino, at least.*

His partner wandered in behind the last crate and

grinned. "I love starting new gigs. Such a sense of hope, so many new things to discover, such a true feeling of partnership and growing friendship with the client."

Jared snorted. "Such a new source of income is what you're really saying."

"Of course."

He laughed. "The move-in seems to be going well, anyway. Let's get stuff unpacked and do our part, too."

Grentham nodded, and they worked together to remove the fronts of the crates to reveal what was inside. The storage units were custom-built, but they'd purchased them from a company that did the gear rock bands used on tour. Everything was neatly arranged and instantly accessible. Jared flipped down a shelf from one of them and pulled out a case that had been behind it, setting it on the horizontal surface.

He popped the latches, opened it to reveal earpieces and glasses, and shook his head. "I'm happy we didn't have to sell the equipment we got from Worldspan. They had some damn fine stuff." Even though their cash flow was currently a mess, once they'd reviewed the items taken from the other security company, there was no question that they would have to keep them. Certain computer-related pieces they'd sent off to Scimitar as part-bribe, part-gesture of goodwill.

Worldspan's communication devices were far, far better than the ones Aces had. They'd already mounted the central control unit in the security station in the other room, and it fed information to the earpieces and the dark sunglasses that lay in the foam container before him. The augmented reality spectacles gave his people in the back the ability to send just about any sort of data display to his people in the field. Jared and Grentham had sacrificed one pair to investigate exactly how they'd managed to get all the technical components required to make the system work into frames that were only slightly larger than normal. The answer was miniaturization and complete optimization of the space, from the tip of the temples to the extra bar over the nose that made them resemble aviator's glasses. He put a pair on, his partner did the same, and they both tucked the earpieces into their ears.

Jared said, "Depending on how this goes, we might have to sell those diamonds. Do you have a plan?"

His partner nodded. "Yeah. I have some out-of-town people who are ready to take them to one of their fences. It'll cost us ten percent off the top, but if they trace them, it won't be to us."

Jared grunted. "You trust them?"

Grentham laughed. "Implicitly. It's my sister's husband."

He looked at his partner quizzically. "I didn't know you had a sister or a brother-in-law."

"As I said, no one can follow the thread back to me. Different mothers and she doesn't acknowledge our father, although she and I have always been reasonably well-connected. She's in California, Hollywood, works in the movies. Magical pyrotechnics."

"Sounds like a fun gig."

He laughed. "She's met Tom Cruise. He wanted to do his stunts, so he put on a fire suit, and she got to hose him down with flame. The insurance company hated it. He loved it."

Jared grinned. "And her?"

"Got an autograph. Said she wouldn't kick him out of bed for snoring."

He shook his head and closed the case, then swapped it with another. This one held small boxes in different pastel colors, each a little smaller than his palm. He asked, "Did we get the testing completed on these?" Jared had been focusing on making new deals while his partner handled integrating the tech they'd stolen and planning the details of their presence at Invention.

The dwarf nodded. "Those little buggers are fantastic. Their detection of explosives is excellent. Strangely, illicit drugs were the least identifiable object. You basically have to be exhaling right into it for it to notice those."

"The traditional stuff?"

"Cameras are high quality, microphones are ridiculously powerful, and there are a couple of extra in the unit specifically to help eliminate room noise, the tech said. He seemed impressed. Proximity is good when activated, and of course, they do fire and smoke and thermal and all the other normal things. Magic detection is a little wonky. Again, better at short range than long."

"Excellent." Jared lowered his voice. "And the extras?"

Grentham laughed and shook his head. "I don't even want to know what they were doing with the capability, but the things were able to read every single cell phone we put in front of them except for the most hardened or encrypted ones. That's with only the wireless, of course. If you add in the cameras, or the microphones, more is possible."

Jared felt a little uncomfortable about collecting that much data from the casino patrons. He'd convinced himself to accept the need based on the fact that a casino had recently crashed to the ground, and thus things could be considered pretty darn serious in Magic City. Grentham continued, "As we agreed, Scimitar will create a bot to analyze the take. If it finds anything suspicious, it'll alert us. If it doesn't, it won't record the data, and we'll never know what it found."

He nodded. It was the most invasive measure he could accept, although he wasn't stupid enough to miss the possibilities. "We both know that puts Scimitar in an excellent position to do what she wants with the data, right?"

His partner shrugged. "Yeah, but we gotta do what we gotta do, right?"

"What we have to do right now is put these things out there. Let's get a move on."

They each collected several devices and headed out to the main area. Jared peeled the adhesive backing off one of the light brown boxes and pushed it against the tan wall outside the door that led backstage to their security area.

A tech's voice reported immediately, "Box Seventeen online. Checks out fully."

Jared replied, "Acknowledged," and headed toward the next logical place to deploy one of the units. When they reached the middle of the floor, Jared paused to examine the space thoroughly. "The mystery floor that we're not allowed on concerns me. Heaven knows what's going on there, and we can't discount the possibility that we might face assault from that direction."

Grentham sighed. "Our external scans don't show any unprotected way onto the floor, so I think it's unlikely. If it makes you feel better, we can add a person at each set of tube lifts. We'll detail four so that one's always on break, and the others rotate from one to the next in, say, fifteen-minute intervals."

Jared nodded. Keeping the security team from getting overly comfortable was key. Even the best got bored and started letting their mind wander after a certain amount of time. "That's all in your capable hands, my friend. While you finish setting things up here, I'll have a chat with the folks at the Kraken. I think they're on the verge of signing up. One more push ought to do it, and telling them about our successful deployment here might be just the thing."

Grentham laughed and slapped him on the shoulder, a reach for the small man. "That's right. Keep your eyes on the money. Go make us a bundle, partner."

Jared shook his head as he headed for the Strip and the short walk to the other casino. *I'm doing my best. Let's hope Julianna Sloane leaves us alone long enough to get things organized before she gives us another "project."*

CHAPTER TWENTY-FIVE

Julianna Sloane watched the feed from a tiny camera hidden in a pin that Thompson wore on her lapel as her lieutenants greeted the principal of Worldspan Security, Angelina Prash, in her building's lobby. The video wasn't particularly crisp, and the audio was tinny as they exchanged pleasantries and offered to escort her upstairs. While they rode up in the elevator, she closed the app on her tablet and set the device aside, then arranged herself on the couch for their entrance.

She had chosen a dark business suit, with a bright golden blouse and a chunky black necklace. Her skirt ended at her knees, and she wore sensible heels. It wasn't overestimating the importance of this meeting to say that many of her plans hinged on it. She had other options, of course, but preferred not to use them if she could instead work with this well-regarded company. She rose at her guest's entrance and shook her hand. The elf looked around the place. "This is quite lovely. If it's all the same to you, I would rather our serious conversation happened on neutral ground."

Her security team frowned as one, and Julianna inclined her head. "Where would you prefer? There are some decent boardrooms downstairs. That's what I usually use for meetings like this," she added, to emphasize she was already giving a lot to the other woman.

The elf nodded. "I understand, and I appreciate that you chose to meet with me here. Still, as they say in the movies, I've been burned before and quite recently, so I'd prefer something a little more public. How about the Ely Strip?"

Prash waved a lazy hand as if expecting a result, and Julianna smiled. "Anti-magic emitter here, I'm afraid. Can't be too careful. If you'd like to head down to the lobby and step outside, we can do it there."

During the elevator ride down, she noted that her security wasn't particularly fond of the idea. She'd seen the hand signals they threw at the camera behind Prash's back, ensuring there would be additional protection waiting outside for them. As they exited the building, the elf created a portal to one end of the Magic City Strip and strode through without a pause. Julianna and her people followed with Smith's and Thompson's hands both inside their jackets on their weapons.

On the other side, Prash waited for several seconds, respecting the possibility that others might join them, then let the rift close. She said, "You have nothing to fear from me. I didn't make it this far in my field by scaring away those interested in doing business with me."

Julianna lifted an eyebrow. "Or by letting them be too comfortable setting the rules."

The other woman laughed, and it seemed a genuinely happy sound. "You're correct. It's very nice to meet someone who understands such things. Some of my potential clients get so upset." She gestured down the Strip and started walking.

Julianna spared a glance to the right, where the owners had cleared the remains of the Mist casino. Nothing remained except a barren plot. *A barren plot that would be mine if they hadn't done such a good job of lawyering up the contract. They're smart bastards, those magicals.*

Prash gestured at the drones flying over the Strip, which were painfully obvious. "It's amateur hour up in here. Pretty sure those are government, although I wouldn't put it past some of the local security companies to have theirs going as well."

"Agreed. It's nice to speak with someone who understands things so clearly, and who has grand ambitions. I think we can accomplish a great deal together."

The elf nodded and scowled at tourists in their path, who moved quickly out of the way. "I'm still unsure why I should work with you. I already have a standing gig here in several of the casinos. Your proposal was enough to inspire curiosity, but really, what's going to make it more worthwhile than what I currently have? As I'm sure you know, the one who requested Worldspan's presence here in the first place is now in charge of the Council."

Julianna kept her face neutral at receiving the unexpected piece of information. "I wasn't aware of that, but it's not particularly relevant. What I have to offer that others do not is simple. Eventually, I will take a large interest in every casino here, from one end of the Strip to the other. A *controlling* interest, in fact." She realized it was the first time she'd ever said the words out loud, although that had been her intent from the beginning. To state them like that was empowering, like a declaration of inevitable success.

Prash responded, "Is that what your husband thought, too?"

Julianna didn't rise to the provocation. *That was beneath you, my friend.* "No, he would've been content with one. In the end, he took one, though not how he intended. I won't be. These bastards will pay, and pay dearly, for taking him from me."

The elf gave a small murmur of assent. "I'm sorry for your loss, by the way."

She nodded. "Thank you. Anyway, I offer a contract to handle security in all of them, in perpetuity, in exchange for helping me achieve my plans. Plus an ownership stake."

The other woman's reply was so fast it seemed automatic. "How much?"

"One percent of profits."

Prash shook her head. "I've worked with enough business owners to know how the books work. One percent of the gross."

Julianna laughed. "Hardly. We can talk specific numbers later once we get the lawyers involved. However, there is a second angle that might appeal to you." The elf smiled. Whether from the banter or the possibility of casino ownership, there was no way to tell. "I'm well aware you were recently humiliated by another security company that attacked your headquarters and blew up your building."

Prash scowled. "That's a carefully guarded secret. One wonders how you know about it."

She ignored the statement. "That had to hurt."

The elf stopped and turned to face her with a hard look, and Julianna matched her. The other woman replied, "It did. I'm aware that they work for you."

She shrugged. "One of many companies we do business with. I didn't order the attack. It was an overstep, and I would've cautioned against it." She admired the way Smith and Thompson both maintained their bored expressions as she lied through her teeth. "I suggest we find a way to do what needs doing in a fashion that scores your revenge on them and not coincidentally gets them out of my hair."

Prash nodded slowly. "What guarantees do I have that this isn't a setup for another attack on my company?"

Julianna shrugged. "You have lawyers. We have lawyers. We'll set up a retainer with significant penalties for any such thing. Put the money in escrow. Whatever."

Conversationally, as if she were doing nothing more than discussing a restaurant menu, the elf said, "Just so you're aware, this is personal for me. Any betrayal would meet with deadly force directed at those in charge, not at their underlings."

Julianna nodded. "Then indeed, we understand one another." She gestured to the side. "Look at that." The elf turned in the direction she'd indicated. Uniformed personnel with the Aces Security logo on their backs were watching people on the Strip, while others installed what looked like additional cameras on the exterior of the Invention casino. "Their footprint in the city is increasing, so there's no time to waste. If you can take over their contracts with the casino and give me an inside resource, so much the better."

Prash nodded and grinned, "Now you're talking."

Angelina portaled back to the company's base, winding up in her office. She exited the room, took the couple of steps to reach her partner's door, and opened it without knocking. He looked up from his desk. "Hey, how goes it?"

She plopped herself down on his couch with a sigh. "The Ely Strip is hot this time of year. Plus, it's filled with oodles of annoying people."

He laughed as he came around from behind his work area and sat in a comfortable chair nearby. "I believe they call those tourists. They're the lifeblood of any gambling operation and also what will pay our bills in that town."

She closed her eyes and leaned her head back against the cushions. "So, the proposal is that we help the widow Sloane take the city for herself, basically. In return, we get to smack down Aces Security and eventually take an ownership stake in their casinos."

He grunted. "Think she's playing fair?"

Angelina shrugged. "I do. I think she's willing to give up a decent amount to get what she wants. At this point, it's less about the money than about payback, which is why she's decided to throw in an ownership stake. Still, it'll be risky."

"Subsidiary corporation then, so nothing blows back on Worldspan?"

She nodded. "If the contract is with the subsidiary, we can later decide what relationship we want to have with the main company. Which means deciding how to handle that ownership percentage will be a lot easier."

He grinned. "You never change, Ang. I love that about you."

"Enough to give me fifty-one percent of our share of the casinos?"

He reached over and slapped her gently on the leg. "No, not *that* much. Fifty-fifty all the way, as always."

She sighed, opened her eyes, and nodded. "I'll have our people check to make sure there's no snake hidden up her sleeve. I think we're about to be doing quite a lot of work in Magic City."

CHAPTER TWENTY-SIX

Angelina walked into her facility's arming room, and pride at the sight of her people getting ready to go struck her. This night's operation would be different than usual since they wouldn't be wearing their normal gear and wouldn't be playing defense. *No, tonight is all about offense.* She clapped her hands for their attention and stood on a nearby stool. "Listen up, people. Our landing location is off the Strip, right next to the target casino. We're going to go in hard. Our main goal is to draw out the principals of the security company for the place, who we've all had the displeasure of meeting before, and get them into the open so we can take them out."

Her second-in-command, a man with a thin dark beard that ran from under his nose down to his jawline and up to his hair, asked, "All the way out?"

"Let me put it this way. I want them to be unable to operate their company for a while. If you can accomplish that by hospitalization, excellent. If you can't, then do what you need to do."

He nodded, a serious expression covering his face. "Got it, boss."

Another person asked, "How big do we want this to be?"

Angelina chuckled inwardly. Brelle was the team's demolition expert, and she could count on the woman to ask that particular question in almost any circumstance. She replied, "The casino should still be standing when we finish. Otherwise, I don't care a bit. If some construction companies get some work out of tonight's adventure, we can always claim we're improving the local economy. Good for PR."

Laughter sounded, and another one of her people commented, "Except for the gnomes and the other security companies, of course."

She replied, "Well, we can offer the gnomes a discount on their contracts to make up for it." She stepped down from the stool and walked through the room, reviewing her people. Roughly three-fourths of them were in the black business suits their recon had spotted the Aces personnel wearing, and the remainder were in fast-made duplicates of the other company's uniforms.

Disguising themselves as their opposition necessarily meant leaving some of their best tools behind, unfortunately. They couldn't bring rifles, for instance. Nothing more than what they could carry in small bags and hidden holsters would do. It wasn't the first time they'd been in such a situation, though, so they had the right people with the right skills, using mostly the right technology. The other company had stolen a bunch of their gear that Worldspan hadn't replaced, not that they would use the best stuff that evening since it was identifiable. *Earpieces yes, glasses no.*

That jogged her memory, and she raised her voice and announced, "Okay, two more things. First, remember to grab the IDs of anyone you take down, along with anything else that might give us access to locked doors and so forth. Pins, watches, whatever. If you have a second to grab it, do it. Don't risk yourselves, of course, because Brelle can always blow any door that's blocking us."

The woman called, "You know it, boss," and laughter sounded.

Angelina continued, "Oh, and if you see any of the tech they stole from us, take it or break it. Thieving bastards."

Her second-in-command observed, "That stuff was insured, right, boss?"

"Of course, and the insurance company has already reimbursed us, which makes it an added benefit if we get it back. Bonuses for everyone. Don't forget our primary objective: the Aces principals go down, and they go down hard. Secondary objective, make sure the gnomes realize how much they need a competent security company."

Her people nodded, and pride filled her at their professional attitude. "All right, warriors. Fifteen minutes to the witching hour. Time to hit the road."

Grentham was enjoying himself with a drink at Grinding Axes, where he was more or less a late-night regular. It was a sort of bar where he didn't expect to see many folks he knew professionally, which suited him fine. Sometimes, he needed time to relax, drink, and people-watch. Even most of his crew didn't know he frequented the place. He enjoyed the anonymity of being another face among the dwarves that patronized it. His phone buzzed, the display reading "unknown," and he lifted it to his ear. Before he could speak, Scimitar's voice snapped, "Put on the glasses."

Adrenaline spiked as he obeyed, and displays blossomed to fill both eyepieces. One displayed the interior of Invention casino, which appeared as it should, full of tourists gambling, drinking, and carousing. The other was from an external camera they'd installed, and it showed a wave of people, dozens of them, dressed in outfits that looked exactly like what his personnel wore. She said, "A bot spotted those. Somehow I don't think they're yours, despite the outfits."

He snarled, "They're not. Sound the alarm at headquarters." He stood and shoved the phone in his pocket, threw a twenty on the table to compensate for the rule he was about to break, and made the social faux pas of opening a portal right there and stepping through to his office. He ran into the locker room to get suited up, strapping on his vest and grabbing a shotgun. His axes were at home where he'd been sharpening them, and he didn't think he could spare the time to retrieve them. *So be it. I'll use magic to burn them down instead, and there's the shotgun for anyone magic won't suffice for.*

Aces people flowed in quickly, and Jared showed up after a couple of minutes and opened his locker to put on his gear. "Know anything more?"

Grentham tapped his ear. "Scimitar says they're inside

and they're causing trouble. She's helping coordinate the response from the team inside."

Jared nodded as he slipped his earpiece in. *You should have had that with you already, chucklehead.* His partner said, "Good," then raised his voice and called to the people in the room, "Anyone who's ready, get over here. You can go over with us. Anyone else, make your way there however you can."

Grentham pulled out his phone and sent a text message. "Some of my most trusted folks will be here soon to act as transport." He opened a portal, and a squad of four ran through it ahead of him and his partner. They pelted down the hallway and broke out onto the gaming floor to find it in complete chaos. Pistols were firing, patrons were shouting, and magic was being thrown all over the place. He cringed involuntarily as lightning blasts slammed into an expensive-looking chandelier with gems resembling gears. It shattered, and the jewels fell to the floor, adding to the frenzy as people scrambled to grab them. He muttered, "Idiots, they're probably fake."

Scimitar spoke, capturing his attention. "Signals from the building have been jammed. Even the wired backup is apparently compromised because there's no police response from the automatic alarm. Also, from the outside, everything looks fine." She opened the window in his glasses. It displayed the take from one of the drones the infomancer had positioned near the Strip at all times since agreeing to work with them. The exterior of the casino looked perfectly normal. He shook his head. "Illusion. Clever bastards. Okay, if things start to go wrong, you can call the cops. Your discretion. Still, wait until it seems like we're not going to win."

The infomancer barked a laugh. "I kinda have doubts already."

Grentham grinned. Despite taking pleasure in the calm and comfortable parts of his life, moments like this were why he kept his hand in the businesses rather than selling out and retiring. "That's because we still have some tricks you haven't seen. Enjoy the show."

He turned to Jared. "Stay safe, partner."

The other man patted the advanced trauma kit that was part of his gear and nodded. "You too. Keep in touch."

Grentham ordered the foursome to accompany his partner, preferring to work solo in the chaos. *Sometimes being shorter than average isn't a bad thing.* He used the gaming tables and structural components of the casino to his advantage, skirting around existing fights, looking for a place where he could make a difference. *Once I figure out who's behind this, if they're here, I'm going to kick their ass up between their ears personally. In the meantime,* his thoughts trailed off as he spotted a fake Aces security person pulling the ID tag off one of his people who was down and bleeding.

He muttered, "I don't think so," and sent a force blast at the man. It caught him entirely by surprise and slammed him into the wall a few feet away. His skull cracked hard against it, and he slumped to the floor on all fours, shaking his head dazedly. Grentham ran over and channeled his momentum into a kick, ensuring that his foe would remain unconscious for some time. *Scumbag.* He knelt and checked the Aces guard, then grabbed the man's first-aid kit and pressed a bandage on the bullet wound in his shoulder. He put the guard's hand on it and pushed, causing him to groan and regain some semblance of consciousness. "Keep the pressure on, right here." He patted his unwounded shoulder. "We'll have a medic look at you as soon as possible. Hang on."

He stood and moved away in a rush, in case anyone had noticed him. Over the comms, he ordered, "Medics, all of them. Quickly. Scimitar, see if you can get the gnomes' medical people out here, too. Extra gear to treat gunshot wounds."

She replied, "On it."

The bark of a pistol from his left announced that someone had spotted him, and he grunted in pain as a bullet plowed into his vest. Their high-end armor was more resistant and channeled less of the impact than the norm, so he got away without any damage to his ribs other than discomfort and probable bruising. He reached down for the shotgun hanging at his side, brought it up with a smile, and pulled the trigger.

He'd loaded it with slugs in case it was necessary to use it as a lock breaker, and the heavy projectile slammed into the man's chest and sent him flying backward to crash onto a blackjack table, knocking it over as he tumbled out of sight behind it. "Serves you right, jerk." Grentham racked the pump to eject the spent shell and position the next. He'd mounted a holder with five more rounds on the weapon's stock, but he doubted he'd find time in the overall frenzy to reload.

Another target of opportunity slipped into view nearby, and he pulled the trigger. That one was a magical and had spotted him at the same time he'd attracted Grentham's notice. The other man called up a force shield, and the angled surface deflected the slug up and away. Then a jet of flame flew at Grentham's face.

He dropped the weapon and created a curved force shield in front of him to deflect the flames. The sprinklers activated since the number of small fires in the room had reached the appropriate level. Grentham laughed, reveling in the pure physicality of the moment, which informed his choice of attack. He rushed at the elf who'd tried to roast him, maintaining his shield and wishing that he'd taken the time to get his axes.

His opponent pummeled him with magical attacks, but none was strong enough to stop his headlong rush. He slammed the shield into the elf, who spun away and went down to one knee on the floor. Grentham let the magic fall and twisted his body into a left hook aimed at the man's temple, which was now right at the perfect height for the punch. It connected, and the elf dropped. He noticed the man's earpiece and cursed as he realized it was identical to his. He said over the comm, "These guys are Worldspan, which probably means they're here because of us. Watch out for the leader, and let me know when you see her. I'm more than happy to give her a rematch." He racked the pump on the shotgun, pushed two more slugs into it, and started hunting for more scumbags.

CHAPTER TWENTY-SEVEN

Morrigan portaled them from the roof of Spirits to the roof of Invention, and Ruby knelt at the edge and peered over while she positioned one of Demetrius' network boosters. "You'd never know anything was happening inside from out on the Strip. Thank goodness Demetrius's programs detected increased encrypted activity here."

Morrigan replied, "Being a casino owner who could call the gnomes to ask what was up didn't hurt either, right?"

She nodded and pointed at the doorway that led into the building, giving Idryll a push to start her moving. "Sometimes things work out how they should. Let's get a move on." They were each in the gear that they could quickly assemble at the bunker, which was most of it. Her knuckles hadn't fully recharged because she'd been busy since she last used them, something that Keshalla would no doubt chide her for if she found out. *Knowing Idryll, she'll find out.*

They smashed the security door barring them from the casino, both Morrigan and Ruby hitting it with force blasts simultaneously. Idryll led the way in her humanoid form, wearing the costume to disguise her identity to free up Ruby's magic for other uses. Between fighting and dealing with the many voices in her head, sometimes concentration proved a problem, and every bit helped.

They quickly found the tube elevators, which Ruby had seen before on a tour of the place but hadn't had the opportunity to use. She slapped another booster, or hack box as she liked to call the devices, on the wall, then jumped in. They delivered her and her partners to the first floor, which was chaos. Security was fighting off an apparent invasion force while patrons screamed and sought safety, but it was hard to tell the teams apart.

Invention's gnome security personnel had assumed that anyone who wasn't of their species and was in a dark suit was fair game. The people in those outfits were squaring off against each other, which meant that choice would probably turn out badly for their contracted security force. *Not my problem.* She reminded, "Nonlethal unless it's life or death. Lots of innocents around here."

She ran over and pressed another box that provided Demetrius with greater access to the casino's electronics onto a nearby wall. Morrigan had already vanished by the time she turned back to Idryll. "Think she's okay?"

The shapeshifter nodded. "She's working through some stuff, you can tell. I have no doubt she'll fight hard."

Ruby muttered, "Not exactly what I was asking," then increased volume and said, "Okay. Let's go see if we can figure out who the bad guys are."

Morrigan had spotted a raised area in the corner, the centerpiece of a circle of slot machines that served as a display holder and advertisement. She blasted herself up to it and kicked the "one dollar" sign off the top, then crouched and reached back for an arrow. It seemed like invaders were still coming in the front doors, so she decided that would be a good spot to begin. She launched the first arrow, knockout gas, and followed it quickly with the second, the one that messed with people's inner ears.

Both flew true and were dispatched on a high enough arc that their origin point was not immediately apparent to those affected by them. Having done what she could to stem the tide flowing into the building, she turned her attention to the melee below. She spotted a single uniformed security guard facing off against two suited attackers and launched a lightning arrow into the middle of the trio. They all writhed under the attack from the electrical magic, then fell to the floor or their knees. The power's dispersal over three people meant that probably none of them would wind up unconscious, but it would at least slow them. Hopefully, someone from the home team would knock the attackers out.

In the far corner of the room, all the way across the space and a challenging shot from her position, she spotted another pair of dark-suited people. They were unloading large backpacks, and Morrigan was pretty sure the things they were pulling out were grenades and mines. Her brain screamed at the danger, and her hands acted without conscious thought, reaching back to select an explosive arrow, putting it to the string, and sending it soaring before she could reconsider.

As it flew, she had the slightest bit of remorse at the damage it might do to the casino, but absolutely none for the duo that was planning to use them against the mixture of combatants and innocents on the gaming floor. The arrow struck and exploded, triggering several of the munitions. The blast wave flew out, shattering glass and slamming people into nearby furniture, breaking some of it. She was sure she'd injured some noncombatants with her action and regretted the necessity. *Better injured than dead from those bastards' grenades, though.*

Her fingers had already found a razor arrow and aimed it at another of the dark-suited attackers shooting into the crowd. She paused and drew a deep breath, thinking that despite being the cause of the explosion, they probably still had enough deniability not to bring the police down on them, especially if Demetrius was able to mess with the camera feeds as he'd once boasted he could. She shifted her aim slightly and set it loose, and the arrow flew to plunge into the forearm holding the pistol and stick there, the arrowhead jutting out the far side of the man's broken arm. He fell to his knees with an expression of great pain and shock, and she grinned with satisfaction. *See, I can shoot without killing. So there, doubters.*

She drew another arrow and looked for a target.

Idryll thrived in the chaotic battle. The sheer number of bodies meant she could get close to her targets before engaging them, and in several cases, she had rendered opponents unconscious from behind before they had any idea they were in danger. Her claws stayed sheathed as she instead relied on speed and the power that momentum provided. While she'd been using her extra musculature quite a lot in the recent past, it wasn't her preference. She was a tiger, and tigers were fast. They struck, faded, and struck again. They *didn't* get into drawn-out punching battles with their enemies. It felt good to be fighting like herself again.

A bulky humanoid in a black uniform, slightly shorter than her, caught her attention because he was using fists and feet to beat anyone who came in range. She wasn't sure why he'd opted to put away his pistol, but since no one else seemed to be targeting him and he was doing quite a bit of damage, she figured he was as good a project as any. She ran toward him, exploiting his current opponent as a sight blocker. Then the security man went down, and the enemy spotted her. He grinned, displaying bloody teeth, and shouted, "Bring it on."

She obliged, running forward and throwing a fist at his face. He seemed to shrink in on himself, bringing his hands in defensively to protect himself from her first flurry of blows. She tried for a knee to his sternum, and he spun suddenly, wickedly fast, bringing his knee around to smash into the side of hers. The pain was intense, the move one she'd never seen before. He continued the spin into a back-fist that slammed into her ribs, and Idryll stumbled sideways.

He hadn't damaged her, but he *had* hurt her, which made her angry. She snarled, "Okay, twinkle toes, you have some good offensive moves. Let's see how you are on defense." She changed her style, darting in with a jab and sliding back, then slapping his hand aside when he tried to counter and going for a joint lock. He yanked hard before she could establish the hold and turned the move into another spin, leaping and bringing his foot around at her head. She cartwheeled to the side to evade it, her skull moving barely ahead of his foot. The moment her feet touched the ground, she lashed out in a front kick. It caught his advancing form right in the stomach and stopped his motion completely.

He coughed once and nodded. "You're a worthy adversary. I'm sorry to have to do this." His hand was a blur as it reached into his jacket in a move she recognized from films galore. Before he could bring the pistol in his shoulder holster to bear, she charged and tackled him, pinning the arm between their bodies. She snapped her head forward and slammed her forehead into his an instant before landing. His momentum plus the force of her strike drove the back of his head into the floor. The gun clattered from nerveless fingers, and she jumped up and searched for a new opponent, already feeling a well-earned headache growing.

Ruby had used subtle magics, mainly force blasts and ropes, to immobilize, daze, and otherwise render unconscious five or six attackers as she moved through the press of people. Demetrius finally spoke in her ear to deliver the information she'd been waiting for. "My algorithm has analyzed the crowd. There are distinct clusters around two individuals."

Ruby nodded. "Those will be the leaders. Let's see them."

An overhead view of the casino floor appeared in a window in her vision, with herself marked in blue, Idryll in orange, and Morrigan in red. Green highlighted another figure, and the last indicator was in yellow. Green was closer to her, so it made the decision easy. "Mo, you've got yellow. Idryll and I will take green."

She performed the mental gymnastics to match up the overhead view with the perspective of her current position. Then she spotted a female elf stalking through the crowd with a pistol in each hand, doing a significant amount of damage beyond what the cohort of guards or cronies around her was putting out. Her face was weird, somehow, and Ruby couldn't make out her features. *Doesn't matter.* "All right, lady. You're contestant number one on tonight's smackdown special."

CHAPTER TWENTY-EIGHT

Morrigan cringed involuntarily as the glass front doors of the Invention casino exploded inward, spreading a shower of shards over the gaming floor. Heavy drones swooped in from the opening, immediately recognizable. She announced, "Paranormal Defense Agency is in the house, going to have to deal with them before I can go after my target," and received curses in response, even from Demetrius. She grinned inwardly. *Now there's a good use for my razor arrows.* The drones were powerful at a distance, but when at short range, had several vulnerabilities. Most glaring were the horizontal propellers that kept them airborne. On the heavier models that used different kinds of engines for propulsion, the ones that helped steer them. Take one of those out, and suddenly whoever was piloting it had a major issue on their hands, assuming the thing didn't instantly crash.

She dispatched an arrow at the nearest without conscious thought, and it buried itself in the armor plating to the side of the propeller. An annoyed growl accompanied the launching of the next, and that one flew true. The propeller snapped, and the drone slewed to the side to slam into another. She laughed at the impact, then cringed when they smashed to the ground near a foursome of fleeing tourists. *Okay, gotta be more careful.*

She selected the drone farthest from endangering any living beings and used an explosive arrow on it. It trailed smoke as it dropped like a rock to land on a pair of still-upright gaming tables. The sprinklers, which were an incredibly annoying feature of the battle, put out the flames immediately. *Well, that's something, anyway.*

A *whirr* sounded as another approached from her left, apparently having spotted her attacking its comrade. She reflexively twisted and pointed her right arm at it, firing the grapnel the agents had given her. The harpoon flew out, and the line got wrapped in the propeller. It yanked her off her perch before she could detach the cable, and she hit the floor and rolled, coming up face-to-face with one of the black-suited attackers.

He looked as shocked as she felt, and she whipped her bow forward, smashing it into his nose and breaking it. She spun into a back kick and sent him flying, then used a blast of force to hurl herself into the air toward the next nearest slot machine pedestal. She landed and cast a veil over herself, then crouched with a razor arrow nocked, waiting to see if anyone had noticed her new position. *Come on, send me another drone. I have a little present for it.*

Scimitar had provided Grentham with directions to the leadership of the invaders. He didn't know how she'd figured it out, and he didn't care. He trusted her implicitly, and once again she'd led him true. A cluster of four individuals fought around a fifth that stayed more or less in the center. They were dressed exactly like his people and used identical weapons, although a couple used two pistols at once, which wasn't policy. If he hadn't been able to recall the faces of each Aces guard, they might have fooled him. *They did a good job of infiltrating, that's for sure. I'm surprised they didn't smuggle in anything heavier, though. Lucky for us, I guess.*

He sent a force blast at the one facing in his direction, knocking the woman upward and back a dozen feet to crash into a nearby wall. He wasn't worried about restraining his attacks. His people had the legal and moral high ground, and thus anything he did in response to the infiltration would be considered reasonable and legitimate. *I love being legitimate. It happens so rarely.* The imposter positioned behind his first target turned to face him and lifted a pair of pistols. He knocked one away with the force blast and threw up a shield to protect himself from the other. He'd drilled the attack and defend routine into his reflexes over countless battles.

The stupidity of that choice occurred to him an instant before the bullet burned into his shoulder outside the vest, twisting him around to the left with the impact's force. *Anti-magic rounds, of course.* He growled and sent a lightning blast at his opponent. A shield flickered into being and withstood his magic for a moment before collapsing beneath his power. "Amateurs." He grabbed a flask from the holder on his belt and downed the healing potion, grimacing as it pushed the bullet out of his body, and the wound knitted itself back together.

Scimitar said, "Interesting news. Someone else is in the system, and the cameras aren't recording."

He frowned. "Why?"

"I presume it's so there's no official record of what goes on here."

"You're recording, right?"

She laughed. "Of course. Also, you should note that the tall person ahead of you is using magic to conceal their features. My systems say it's a woman, based on body measurements."

The woman's face was shifting subtly, meaning that whatever look she was wearing at a given moment in time wasn't her real one. She dispatched blasts of magic at a pair of gnomes, sending them flying. *I recognize that body language.* He called, "Hey, wench. I hoped we'd find each other. Good to see you again."

The woman turned, and a smile spread over her face. She replied, in a familiar voice, "I've been looking for you."

———

Ruby dashed across the floor, following Demetrius's directions toward the leader marked in green, and saw the tall figure turn to face a dwarf. It took her a second to realize it was Grentham, and she chided herself for not anticipating that. *You're reacting, not thinking, Ruby. Get it together.* The tall person had two associates guarding them, and Ruby threw a line of force out at the one on her right, then yanked them forward. The move put them directly in the way of the other, who shifted his pistols out of line barely in time to avoid perforating his partner.

She used the instant of the rear one's obscured vision to throw herself into the air, hurtling over the middle defender and kicking out her feet at the far one. The double-footed blow knocked them back toward the one in the center, who moved adroitly away without abandoning her focus on Grentham. Now that she was closer, Ruby could see that the tall person was a woman and was disappointed to find it wasn't the Drow she'd thought it might be. *Again, not a smart hope since this action is harming magicals, but you never know.*

She turned and used force blasts to knock the guns out of the other guard's hands, then skipped close and snapped a punch into his face. He swung back at her, and she blocked hard enough to fracture his forearm, then spun and cut his legs out from underneath him. He slammed onto the ground, and she reached out with her force magic to grab a fallen Taser, probably one of the real security guards' weapons. She shot the downed man and discharged the voltage into him, taking him from dazed to unconscious. She let the weapon drop and turned to deal with the person in charge.

The woman's face was morphing, a clever disguise that would wreak havoc on facial recognition software. *I need to figure out how to do that and keep it going while I do other stuff. That's clever.* She had abandoned any pretense of being human and was firing magic at the dwarf, who had wrapped himself in a force shield that kept him safe but also prevented him from attacking. The woman said something about being able to last longer than him this time. Fortunately, nothing was holding Ruby back from engaging her.

She dashed in and planted a pair of quick punches into the figure's lower back. Her opponent straightened with a howl and spun faster than Ruby would've expected, smashing a forearm in at her head. Ruby blocked it, and it knocked her stumbling to the side from the sheer force. *Okay, she's pumping her muscles. Two can play at that game.* Ruby threaded magic into her body as she found her balance and called to the dwarf, "Maybe do something other than cowering under your shield? Sometime today, perhaps?"

He replied, "Yeah, whatever. Why the hell did you punch her instead of blasting her to pieces?" However, his protection fell, and he threw a blast of fire at their common foe.

Ruby charged in again, the woman now using one hand to alternately shield and throw magic at the dwarf to keep him pinned down and the other to hurl shadow blasts at Ruby. She ducked and dodged on her way in, deflecting some of them with a buckler of force on her left arm. With a burst of speed, she went in for a kick, only to have to veer off when her foe created a pillar of flame right in her path. The evasion took her near the dwarf. "You're not doing a great job of protecting the place, I've gotta say. Your Yelp! reviews are going to be terrible."

The snarl in his voice was evident, despite the cacophony around them. "Not all of us can choose our battles so we look good. I bet you stand in front of the mirror admiring yourself daily, fancy-ass dragon head."

Not daily. Weekly, maybe. Ruby had to dive and roll away from a particularly vicious blast of shadow aimed at both of them, and when she came up, the woman had summoned force blades in both hands and was backing away to keep both her and Grentham in sight. Ruby drew her sword, opening her mind to let its inhabitants in, and charged at the woman. She noted in her peripheral vision that Grentham was circling, trying to get behind their opponent, and shook her head. *Sure, let me be the bait. Bastard.*

Idryll finished taking down one of the invaders and looked up to see a flood of PDA agents coming through the door. She was positive she and her friends were targets as much as anyone else in the place, so she crouched and moved away under cover of the few gaming tables that still stood. A pair of elves in dark suits suddenly blocked her path. They attacked immediately upon noticing her. Each carried a pair of batons, probably liberated from fallen guards, that sparked at the ends. *Stun weapons. Smart.*

She circled to the left to prevent simultaneous attacks from both and said into the comm, "We have PDA agents here now in addition to the drones. I doubt they'll make distinctions between the good guys and the bad guys. Not to mention the fact that they're seriously confused about which ones we are." Then she had to focus on the fight, and everything else faded into the background.

The nearer elf swept the baton around at head height, displaying absolutely no realization of how fast she was. To be fair, she'd not been moving at top speed. She did now, whipping out a hand to grab his wrist and pivoting to slam her other fist into his tricep. His arm offered less resistance as it went numb, and she spun underneath it, wrenching it up behind him. He stood on his tiptoes, and she pushed forward with all her substantial strength, sending him tripping toward his partner.

The other elf danced out of the way in a quick spin, and Idryll nodded in appreciation of his show of agility. She'd come out of the previous exchange with the baton in her hand, having grabbed it unconsciously as she made her move, and she threw it at her foe. He brought his across to block it, then advanced cautiously. He flicked the baton out at her, and she leaned back the minimum distance to avoid it. She needed to stay near, as the weapons gave him the advantage of a longer reach. He was wisely keeping one close to his body, and she couldn't risk having him block a punch with it because the shock might slow her enough to give him an opportunity.

She feinted inward, and he shifted the baton in a short block, refusing to over commit. She stutter-stepped to the side, and he lunged forward, almost catching her. He extended far enough that she was able to snap a foot up into his ribs, and while he lurched away sufficiently quickly to avoid having anything broken, she saw in his eyes that the blow had hurt him. Then she dove aside as a PDA drone strafed across their fight, stitching the other man and his partner with bullets and narrowly missing her. She ran from the drone, shouting, "Watch out, they're shooting to kill."

CHAPTER TWENTY-NINE

As she deflected a strike from the woman's sword, Ruby said to the dwarf, "The damn stupid scumbag PDA is here. I hate those guys." She and he were side by side, harrying their shared enemy.

Grentham replied, "You know, they've jacked into the self-driving cars." He blocked an attack from the woman and countered with a stuttering line of fire bolts, but she easily intercepted it with her force blade.

"I didn't know that. One more reason to dislike them."

"Magic City issues should remain with Magic City people."

Ruby replied, "Right? That's what I've been saying." The enemy charged at her, moving to the opposite side of where the dwarf was and slashed as she went past. Ruby blocked the first sword with the tip of hers and the second with the blade near the pommel, then snapped out a kick. The woman twisted away, and Ruby decided she had to be an elf based on her impressive agility and height.

She turned to stay engaged with their foe, trusting that

Grentham wouldn't attack her from behind while they had a common enemy. They traded a series of thrusts and blocks. Her foe said, "You know, there's no way you can make a difference on your own. Maybe we should join forces."

Ruby brought a chop around at the woman's arm, hoping to wound her enough to take away one of her paired weapons. *Maybe Keshalla's right and I should keep pushing to master the double sword. Then I'll need to get another artifact blade, and it'll be a whole big thing. And I'm so busy already.* She laughed at her nonsense. "Yeah, no, I don't think so. You seem like a part of the problem rather than the solution."

Morrigan's voice snapped, "Jewel, three o'clock, incoming." Her sister had taken to using the call signs most of the time. She and Idryll were still having problems making that a habit. Ruby immediately covered herself in a force cocoon and twisted toward the designated direction. A grenade was sailing in, launched by someone in a PDA uniform holding a combination rifle and grenade launcher, and she deflected it off to the side with a burst of magic. It exploded, and she realized the agents weren't very particular about collateral damage at the moment. *Probably figure they can blame it on us.* She shook her head and called, "Okay, short stuff. I guess you'll have to finish the skinny trash queen on your own. Good luck." She dashed toward the man with the launcher.

Morrigan drew a bead on one of the PDA soldiers who faced away from her, aiming for the center of his backpack. She'd lost the chance to get to the leader Ruby had chosen for her. That person was no longer traceable, according to Demetrius, so now she sought targets of opportunity. She selected a magic arrow that delivered a force blast upon impact, thinking it should knock him into the one next to him and send that one into a couple more. The geometry felt properly laid out, like a trick shot in billiards, which she was pretty good at. She released the arrow with a smile on her face and watched it speed across the distance in a matter of seconds. It struck precisely where she intended it to and ultimately failed to do anything more than bounce off. She spat a curse and announced, "The backpacks are anti-magic emitters, and they're active."

Demetrius swore as his worry escaped him momentarily, something he rarely did. Ruby replied, "Nothing we haven't faced before. I'm on my way after one, do what you can." She reached for a razor arrow, lacking any technological options that weren't explosive, then sighed. *I can't put bladed arrows into federal agents. That's crossing a line we won't be able to come back from.*

She pressed the button to collapse the bow and shoved it into her holster. Using her pistol or her daggers risked the same issues as the razor arrows, so she leapt off her pedestal, ran to the nearest downed security guard, and grabbed a pair of stun batons lying beside him. *No arrows, no daggers. Honestly, this hero thing is way too restrictive.* She spotted a couple of people in Aces uniforms as they crept around the periphery of the battle with their guns raised, looking for targets. Their posture and the looks on their faces spoke of predatory behavior, not the responsibility and defensive focus she'd expect to see in the casino's protectors.

She charged in under a veil, materializing as she smacked the batons down on both of their gun hands, sending one weapon to the floor and the other one flying through the air. They quickly recovered from their shock at her appearance, the one on the left a beat faster than his partner as he threw a punch at her face. The man stepped into the blow, causing her to lean back so far to avoid it that she had to turn the move into a backflip. She regained her balance and stared at the pair, who hadn't pursued. The one on the right was clawing at something on his belt and came up with a Taser. A laugh escaped before she realized that without the ability to shield herself, the weapon had reasonable potential for harm.

She threw her stick on that side at his face, forcing him to focus on defending against it rather than bringing the Taser to bear, and attacked the other. She slammed an elbow at his temple, and when he blocked it, jammed the stun baton in his torso. He got an arm in the way, but it still made contact with the shock head of the weapon, and he jittered before falling away. The first had regained his equilibrium and fired at her. She couldn't evade the tines, and they stabbed through her costume, which didn't include the protective vest because they'd deployed so quickly. She stiffened as the voltage coursed through her, then collapsed to the floor as her muscles told her brain they weren't interested in anything it might have to say.

Grentham wished again that he had his axes if only for the poetic closure they would offer to this rematch with the woman. He taunted, "Decided your face was too horrible to show? Were you burned? Did the explosion get you?"

She shook her head, and a smile grew on the parade of faces that moved across her visage. "No, I want to be sure that when they look at the security footage, they can't identify who it is. Because they'll think it was you all, and your company's going down."

He threw a bolt of fire at her face and another immediately after at her legs, hoping that one or the other would connect. She danced away from them both, frustratingly competent. The woman had given up her swords when the costumed weirdo left, returning to a magic-on-magic battle. She dodged and attacked. He attacked and summoned shields to block. They were fairly evenly matched, him tougher and her more nimble, although he couldn't help but think she had something of a home-field advantage, having planned to be at the casino tonight as opposed to getting drawn in without warning.

Scimitar's voice interrupted unexpectedly, talking in that chopped fashion she used during tense moments. "Been analyzing people's movements. Clusters are forming around you and J." She only ever referred to them by their initials over comm. "I think it's a trap."

Grentham's adrenaline level jumped through the roof. If the objective had been to bring them out, it had worked. If the further plan had been to separate them, that had worked, too. *Holy hell, we played right into their hands from step one.* For an instant, he wondered if Worldspan had lost the battle at their headquarters on purpose to set this moment up, but then he rejected that idea. *Nope, too para-noid. They would've killed us there if that was their intent, or at least tried a lot harder. This tastes like revenge.* He summoned a wall of flame, one of his most powerful spells, setting it between him and the elf woman, then ran in the opposite direction. "Where is he?"

Scimitar guided him into position, and he found Jared and one guard being manipulated into a corner by a series of magical attacks. He brought up his shotgun on the run and blasted the two he had clean shots at. The third spun, bringing his hands up defensively, then pitched forward and fell. Jared was behind him, the pistol held at head level smoking. Grentham said to his partner, "This is about us. We need to get out of here."

Jared nodded. "Lead the way." Grentham summoned a portal, and they both ran through it before any of the PDA losers with their anti-magic backpacks, which he had recognized immediately upon seeing them, could intervene.

Idryll finished tying up the one who'd knocked down Morrigan and asked her for the fifth time if she was okay. The woman growled at her and swore that if she didn't go away right then, she'd make her life a living hell for the next month. Idryll took that as confirmation that their partner was fine and ran toward Ruby, who was just finishing rendering a Paranormal Defense Agency agent unconscious. She ripped a rifle out of his loose grip and threw it across the room.

As Idryll arrived, more noise came from the entrance, and a bunch of people in military-style gear flooded in, along with uniformed members of the Ely Police Department. Ruby growled, "You've got to be kidding me. Worldspan security, now? I thought someone ran them out of town."

Idryll gestured toward the back of the casino. "Maybe it's time for us to fade away. Looks like this is going to wrap up pretty soon." She moved in that direction, and Ruby followed.

Her partner said, "I don't see the point of it. Was this only to make the casino security look bad? Or something deeper?"

"That would be a lot of effort for a minimal reward. It has to be part of a bigger game. Maybe it all went wrong when the PDA showed up."

Ruby nodded. "Yeah, could be. If they hadn't, and we hadn't, it would be a smack in the face, demonstrating Aces' ineptitude. It seems like the PDA makes *everything* worse." She stopped in her tracks, and Idryll turned to face her. "You know, I think it's time to do something about that. I'll need your help."

Ruby laid out the plan, and Idryll ran to do her part. Demetrius vectored them in on Paul Andrews, who was leading from the front. *I can respect that about him, at least. Although he's probably doing it out of the desire to harm rather than any noble instinct.* He had four others with him, and Idryll jumped to the top of a nearby slot machine and launched herself toward them. They scattered as people tended to do when a screaming person suddenly flew at them, and Ruby threw the EMP at the PDA leader.

Idryll landed and twisted as it went off, intending to go to her partner's side. Ruby cast a wall of force to separate Andrews from his support people. Intentionally or not, it also separated Ruby from the tiger-woman. She watched through the translucent barrier as her partner cast a portal and tackled Andrews through it. At the last instant, the man's sidekick leapt through, clearing the edge as it closed. Idryll mastered the anger that flowed through her at her partner's decision to yet again go it alone and started rehearsing the words she was going to scream at her when they were next together.

Morrigan's voice came over the comms. "Come on, Cat. Time to get the hell out of this mess. Probably the Army will show up next. Or a marching band. No way to tell, this kind of night."

CHAPTER THIRTY

Ruby landed on top of Andrews in the receiving room in her bunker, with small fixtures set in the sides and the ceiling dimly lit. She rose to her feet and retreated to the corner to await his reaction to being portaled away. She hadn't anticipated another PDA goon coming along, but neither was she worried about it. This was her place, and she had all the advantages. She could take them both out with magic, but that was too easy, and the purpose of this little adventure was to teach them a lesson.

Andrews stood slowly, then convulsively moved as he went for the pistol in his holster. She reached out with her force magic, ripped it from his hand, and used her power to bend the barrel, rendering it too dangerous to use. She let it fall and plucked the woman's from her holster and repeated the process. He snarled, "So, what, now you're going to kill us? I knew I was right about you all."

Ruby shook her head. "Don't be ridiculous. If I'd wanted to kill you, I would've done it there. It's time we came to an understanding. I sense you lack respect because you think everything impressive about me is magical. So, you know, give it your best shot. I can take you without magic."

His subordinate asked, "You're kidding, right? Are we in the schoolyard or something?"

Ruby shrugged. "I tried this once the grown-up way. Showed up to have a calm conversation. What I got instead was an elaborate trap. So, if you all want to be children, we'll play by children's rules."

Andrew said, "You took away our weapons."

"That I did. I won't use any either. Plus, there are two of you to one of me. Of course, you could accept the truth that your fear of magicals is clouding your judgment and negatively influencing your actions."

The woman shook her head. "How does a fistfight accomplish that?"

Ruby sighed. "Probably it won't. Frankly, I'm out of other ideas with you people. I could kill you out of hand, but I don't need the federal nonsense that would bring down. I could portal you to the World In Between, but that seems exceptionally cruel, even given your transgressions." Their eyes widened, indicating they had at least some knowledge of the horrific landscape that existed in some indeterminate space connected to both Earth and Oriceran, but hadn't considered she might know how to access it.

She was silent for almost a minute while thoughts ran through her head, and apparently, she'd scared them enough that they feared to interrupt. Finally, she said, "When I brought you here, I thought you deserved a beating. Payback for the garbage you've done if nothing else. I still think that, but I also believed a demonstration of non-magical power might influence you. It won't, will it?"

Their expressions provided the answer to that question. She shook her head in frustration. "You know, I don't get you people. Supposedly your job is to stand up for the little guy, but it seems like all you do is try to control the little guy. I've seen other government organizations, and they don't behave that way. Which means *you* are the problem." Andrews flinched at that, and she shouted, "Don't you move, or so help me, I will both beat you down *and* throw you broken into the World In Between." He froze, apparently believing the lie. *I really, really hope it's a lie. Might be Morrigan's not the only one with mental baggage at the moment.*

She mastered her anger. "So, here's the thing. You saw evidence tonight that my companions and I are not a threat to Magic City. We're here to help." She put one hand on her hip and pointed at Andrews with the other. "I'm giving you exactly three options to choose from. First, and best, you get the hell out of my town and take all your people with you. We didn't ask for your help, and we don't need it."

He scowled and shook his head. "You're delusional."

She cut him off. "Shut up, dumbass. I'm speaking. Second, not so good, you stay, but you keep your focus where it belongs. That means away from me and mine, and actually investigating things, rather than only throwing a surveillance net around everything so you can show up to deliver fictitious justice to some magicals whenever the opportunity presents itself."

Now the woman sputtered, and Ruby turned a glare on her. "You also shut up. I get the idea you all think that magicals are bad or dangerous by definition. We're no more of each than any human. We simply have different tools. Some people use drones, for instance. I can't imagine how much the damage you caused tonight will cost to repair, and there are some kinds of harm that aren't fixable. You all are every bit as reckless and uncaring as the worst magicals I've ever met.

"Now third—and I think you should *really* consider not selecting this option—you keep doing what you're doing. If that is your decision, you should know that the hands-off approach I've been taking to your overly invasive tactics in my town is over. You're way past the line, and you have gained my complete attention. I am more than happy to knock you back to the proper side of it as painfully as possible. So, choose wisely."

Without giving them a chance to respond, she created a portal at their backs and blasted them through it with bolts of force, sending them into the desert near the abandoned motel that was now only fire-blackened wood. Right before the rift closed, she tossed a microphone transmitter through, tiny enough that they wouldn't notice it. Her earpiece carried their voices across the distance.

Andrews said, "Damn her. Damn them all." He was shouting at the end of the sentence. Ruby laughed at his angst.

His companion replied, "Are you going to do it, boss? Are we leaving?"

His voice was dark. "Hell no. They're going down."

Ruby sighed as he made the choice she'd expected but hoped he wouldn't. *Okay. Option three it is.*

The next night, Ruby sat to dinner with her housemates and a couple of guests. Morrigan, who had already become fast friends with Shiannor, sat at her left, and Idryll sat to her right. She'd explained that one was her sister and the other was her companion, who would be rooming with her occasionally now. Liam asked, "Does this mean you and Demetrius are over?"

Ruby laughed. "Hardly." She rose and gave the man in question a giant kiss on the lips. Hoots and howls sounded in response.

Daphne announced, "I have good news as well. I resigned from the Ebon Dragon to pursue my magic full time." Loud applause greeted her words, and she gave a small bow. "That means I'll be around more, and if you are all okay with it, I'll kick in a little extra toward rent if you'll let me use the place as my business center."

They all agreed and shared a great meal Ruby had brought from her favorite restaurant in Spirits. When they were in the kitchen afterward, Ruby having volunteered Morrigan to help her clean up, her sister asked, "Everything all right?"

She shrugged. "The PDA has decided not to back down, so we're going to have to take them on. Plus, the Drow worries me."

Morrigan sighed. "I get that. At least our opposition seems clear now."

"I'd like to believe that, but you know what? As soon as you start believing that, life kicks you in the teeth and shows you that what you think is true really isn't." The vehemence in her tone came as a surprise even to her.

Morrigan's voice softened. "Well, sister, one thing will always be true where you and I are concerned."

Ruby stopped washing dishes and turned her head to look at her sister. "What is that?"

The other woman put her hand on her shoulder and said, ever so softly, "I will always be prettier and smarter and more interesting than you."

She smashed a handful of soap suds into her sister's mouth, and they started slap-fighting as they'd done when they were children, howling with laughter. A moment later, Idryll came in from the other room and froze at the sight of them. The shapeshifter shook her head. "Honestly. Most immature *Mirra* ever." She turned and stalked out of the room, leaving Morrigan and Ruby laughing all the harder.

Elnyier was in the private room of Void, Darkest Night casino's best restaurant. Having the space at her disposal was one of the privileges of being the casino's majority owner. She had two aides at her sides, both Drow, a male and a female. They took furious notes as she spun out ideas while occasionally pausing for small bites of her appetizer course. "We're going to need to change the decorations in the palace, for one. Maldren had no taste whatsoever. Have a selection of fabrics for me tomorrow. Also, I'll need to meet with each Council member individually. Please arrange it."

They scribbled, and she took another bite, then set the fork down as she sensed an additional presence in the room. "Also, talk to the heads of security at each casino, see what concerns they have. Use intermediaries. I don't want anyone to know it's me, but I'm not sure the owners are as clued in on things as they ought to be. Let's build our sources whenever possible. Now, you can go."

If either was offended at the brushoff, they didn't show it, only left professionally, almost bowing on the way out. She stared at the shadows where she thought the presence was. "I wondered when you'd make contact. I hear a lot about your activities in town."

The Drow male Dieneth, who she'd met once before at the casino, materialized as his veil faded. He grinned. "You disapprove?"

She shrugged. "I think you could be more effective. I might be able to help you with that." She gestured at the chair next to her, and he accepted the invitation to sit.

"Why do you believe it's me who's stirring things up? I'm only here to pay proper respects to the new Lady of the kemana."

She laughed. "I don't *believe* it's you. I *know* it's you. I have eyes and ears everywhere, my friend. Very little goes on in the city that I'm not aware of."

He plucked one of the tempura shrimp from her plate with his fingers and popped it into his mouth. "The benefits of being on the Council, I suppose."

Elnyier shook her head. "No, I'm smart enough to have separate networks, thank you very much. So, are you willing to step up your game?"

"Perhaps, if the price is right. Why? What would you get out of the deal?"

"Power. Influence. The usual." Her long fingers reached over and rested on his hand. She put a little seduction in her voice. "Maybe more, if you're interested."

He grinned, and she noted again that he was very handsome, as she'd thought the first time they'd met, years before. "I'm quite interested in power, influence, and," he paused long enough to be sassy, "more."

She laughed deep in her throat. "Excellent. Will you have some wine?" It was clearly an invitation for more than a drink.

His smile conveyed his understanding of all that she offered. "I'd love to."

Ruby's story doesn't end here. Continue her and her friend's adventures in *DARKNESS ASCENDANT*.

THANK YOU!

Stay up to date on new releases and fan pricing by signing up for my newsletter. CLICK HERE TO JOIN.

Or visit: www.trcameron.com/Oriceran to sign up.

If you enjoyed this book, please consider leaving a review.

Thanks!

AUTHOR NOTES - TR CAMERON

MAY 20, 2021

Thank you for reading Book 6 in the Magic City Chronicles, and for continuing on to read these author notes! Ruby completed the Venamisha earlier than I expected at the start of the series, but it felt right for her to do it at this moment.

I've transitioned into summer mode, which for me is almost like moving to a different reality. Still a ton of responsibility all around, but it shifts from one area to the other. My kid and I drove North to visit my best friend, and he took us hiking so we could finish a hiking patch. It was possibly the most brutally exhausting thing I've ever done – and for him, it was a comparatively tiny mountain.

And the kid was not happy in the slightest. They do a great job of not devolving into whining and complaining mostly, but this one stressed us both out. But we survived, and now anytime they're upset I can say, "But you survived the mountain! This is nothing."

The parents reading this know exactly how well that goes over, but I'm a Dad, and it's my job to be annoying.

I've started the preproduction process on Rogue Agents of Magic. I'm very excited to return to that part of my little corner of the Oriceran Universe, and the story is coming together well.

Civilization VI continues to be beyond addictive. I bought the expansion and am really liking it. Again, no one hoping to get anything else done should play it. I've discovered the board game "Space Base," and I adore it. Just the right amount of brainpower required. Getting back into board gaming is one of my goals for the summer. We've got a couple other ones on the shelf that we've never played, including a Sherlock Holmes cooperative one that I'm eager to try.

My other media use is all over the place right now. I'm still listening to the audiobook of *Sandman*, which is amazing. *Star Trek: Discovery* is great; I'm almost done with Season 1. The kid and I returned to the theatre to see a movie, winding up with *Raya and the Last Dragon*, which was phenomenal. *Flight Attendant* is interesting, but depressing. And *Castlevania* is back, which is awesome!

A visit to our local amusement park is in the offing for next week, and I'm still working on the epic summer trip. We'll see how that goes.

I'm hoping to find the time to learn the guitar via Rocksmith, or possibly pick up an electronic drum kit and start to learn that. I really like the idea of banging the drums as catharsis, but I don't know if I have the patience and brain power to teach myself how to play. And I know I don't have the dedication right now to spend money to learn. So, if you're reading this and you know how to learn to play drums, find me on Facebook and share your wisdom!

For the series after RAM, I'm thinking of something involving monsters. Seems like a magical world like Oriceran would have a lot of wicked monsters to deal with, some of which would doubtless spill over to Earth...

Before I go, once again, if this series is your first taste of my Urban Fantasy, look for "Magic Ops." I promise you'll enjoy it, and you'll get more of Diana, Rath, and company. You might also enjoy my science fiction work. All my writing is filled with action, snark, and villains who think they're heroes. Drop by www.trcameron.com and take a look!

Until next time, Joys upon joys to you and yours – so may it be.

PS: If you'd like to chat with me, here's the place. I check in daily or more: https://www.facebook.com/AuthorTRCameron. Often I put up interesting and/or silly content there, as well. For more info on my books, and to join my reader's group, please visit www.trcameron.com.

If you enjoyed this book, please consider leaving a review. Thanks!

The new garden is currently being built in the back of the Dream House. The design takes up the entire backyard and the two sides of the house. There's a new steel pergola and the patio size doubled and there's raised beds and an arch and bench and a water feature and a few other things I keep forgetting to mention. Plus peach trees and fig trees and shade trees and blueberry bushes and raspberry bushes and more. Café lights around the pergola and lighting down one side of the yard. The details kind of go on and on but you get the idea. It's gonna be the bomb!

The goal was to create my own Secret Garden. When someone comes in the back gate, I want them to forget where they are for a moment. A retreat in the suburbs of Austin.

The idea has always been in the back of my mind. Once I had the dream house and had done a lot to the interior, it was time to look to the other part of the property.

I was also helped along by Covid and quarantine. It was more important than ever to squeeze out every bit of serenity and use that I could from every square inch. That was last June.

Apparently, I was not alone in my thinking and everyone was looking to turn their backyard into a safe place to meet with neighbors.

Here we are a year later and the dream is getting made into a reality. The good dog Lois Lane and the sweet pittie Leela are not so sure about it. They've been consigned to staring out the back door without being able to go out there. Potty breaks for now are on a leash in the front yard. At 2:30 in the morning no one is thrilled about it but I did get to see the red moon this time – a few times.

First they took out the top five inches of top soil to get everything ready. Then, right on cue the clouds appeared and the rains began – for a week. To their credit, Native Edge landscapers worked through the week emerging from the backyard covered in mud and slowly but surely the backyard has been transforming.

Out front there's a long, large stack of black slate and the driveway is full of two kinds of dirt. Not sure what that's about. I can see the neighbors walking by from my office window, bending and twisting trying to get a better view of the backyard.

Surely that much black African slate and giant piles of dirt has to be adding up to something magnificent.

Mine is not even the biggest redo in my neighborhood. Thanks to humble brag pics on Facebook I've gotten a peek at what the Jones' are doing. There are a lot of new pools around here that are in a variety of shapes with fire pits and outdoor kitchens and pergolas and new gardens. Amazing.

My little bit of paradise will be finished in a few weeks and there will be plenty of pictures on Facebook. Plus on July 4th a party with a seafood boil to celebrate surviving cancer for the 5th time, getting vaccinated and out on the town, the 4th of course, and the inauguration of the new garden. I've even rented a Slurpee machine. Red punch and orange mango flavors.

If anyone's looking for me, I can be found among the trees sitting on my bench sipping a Slurpee. Party on people. More adventures to follow.

If you enjoyed this book, you may also enjoy the first series from T.R. Cameron, also set in the Oriceran Universe. The Federal Agents of Magic series begins with Magic Ops and it's available now at Amazon and through Kindle Unlimited.

FBI Agent Diana Sheen is an agent with a secret...

...She carries a badge and a troll, along with a little magic.

But her Most Wanted List is going to take a little extra effort.

She'll have to embrace her powers and up her game to take down new threats,

Not to mention deal with the troll that's adopted her.

All signs point to a serious threat lurking just beyond sight, pulling the strings to put the forces of good in harm's way.

Magic or mundane, you break the law, and Diana's gonna find you, tag you and bring you in. Watch out magical baddies, this agent can level the playing field.

It's all in a day's work for the newest Federal Agent of Magic.

Available now at Amazon and through Kindle Unlimited

OTHER SERIES IN THE ORICERAN
UNIVERSE:

THE LEIRA CHRONICLES
SOUL STONE MAGE
THE KACY CHRONICLES
MIDWEST MAGIC CHRONICLES
THE FAIRHAVEN CHRONICLES
I FEAR NO EVIL
THE DANIEL CODEX SERIES
SCHOOL OF NECESSARY MAGIC
SCHOOL OF NECESSARY MAGIC: RAINE CAMPBELL
ALISON BROWNSTONE
FEDERAL AGENTS OF MAGIC
SCIONS OF MAGIC
THE UNBELIEVABLE MR. BROWNSTONE
DWARF BOUNTY HUNTER
CASE FILES OF AN URBAN WITCH

OTHER BOOKS BY JUDITH BERENS

OTHER BOOKS BY MARTHA CARR

JOIN THE ORICERAN UNIVERSE FAN GROUP ON FACEBOOK!

BOOKS BY MICHAEL ANDERLE

Sign up for the LMBPN email list to be notified of new releases
and special deals!

https://lmbpn.com/email/

For a complete list of books by Michael Anderle, please visit:

www.lmbpn.com/ma-books/

CONNECT WITH THE AUTHORS

TR Cameron Social

Website: www.trcameron.com

Facebook: https://www.
facebook.com/AuthorTRCameron

Martha Carr Social

Website: http://www.marthacarr.com

Facebook: https://www.facebook.com/
groups/MarthaCarrFans/

Michael Anderle Social

Website: http://lmbpn.com

Email List: http://lmbpn.com/email/

Social Media:

https://www.facebook.com/LMBPNPublishing

https://twitter.com/MichaelAnderle

https://www.instagram.com/lmbpn_publishing/

https://www.bookbub.com/authors/michael-anderle

CPSIA information can be obtained
at www.ICGtesting.com
Printed in the USA
BVHW031129130621
609464BV00018B/312